WELCOMING COMMITTEE

Morgan was looking almost directly at the window when he saw the blossom of smoke. It came from across the street and the sound of the shot echoed as he saw the President stumble. The .44 Colt was in Morgan's hand instantly and he sent five shots into the window as fast as he could pull the trigger.

A great shout went up from the crowd, women screamed and Morgan was into the street, running for the row of buildings on the far side. A half dozen police were running with him and one shouted. They piled into the stairway and clattered up to a hall . . . and halted.

In the hallway was the body of a man. He was half in and half out of a doorway. There was a rifle on the floor behind him.

He had got the assassin—but the President was dead. Morgan was certain of it.

RIDE THE TRAIL TO RED-HOT ADULT WESTERN EXCITEMENT WITH ZEBRA'S HARD-RIDING, HARD-LOVING HERO...

SHELTER
by Paul Ledd

#18: TABOO TERRITORY	(1379, $2.25)
#19: THE HARD MEN	(1428, $2.25)
#22: FAST-DRAW FILLY	(1612, $2.25)
#23: WANTED WOMAN	(1680, $2.25)
#24: TONGUE-TIED TEXAN	(1794, $2.25)
#25: THE SLAVE QUEEN	(1869, $2.25)
#26: TREASURE CHEST	(1955, $2.25)
#27: HEAVENLY HANDS	(2023, $2.25)
#28: LAY OF THE LAND	(2148, $2.50)
#29: BANG-UP SHOWDOWN	(2240, $2.50)

Available wherever paperbacks are sold, or order direct from the Publisher. Send cover price plus 50¢ per copy for mailing and handling to Zebra Books, Dept. 2340, 475 Park Avenue South, New York, N.Y. 10016. Residents of New York, New Jersey and Pennsylvania must include sales tax. DO NOT SEND CASH.

WHISTLESTOP WENCH #30
SHELTER

BY
PAUL
LEDD

ZEBRA BOOKS
KENSINGTON PUBLISHING CORP.

ZEBRA BOOKS

are published by

Kensington Publishing Corp.
475 Park Avenue South
New York, NY 10016

Copyright © 1988 by Paul Ledd

All rights reserved. No part of this book may be reproduced in any form or by any means without the prior written consent of the Publisher, excepting brief quotes used in reviews.

First printing: April, 1988

Printed in the United States of America

CHAPTER ONE

Slipping the Colt revolver from its holster, Shelter Morgan walked along the side of the corral. It was a dark night with only a sliver of moon visible. Pausing in the deep shadow of one of the two huts, he opened the loading gate, pulled the hammer to half cock and slid a sixth cartridge into the cylinder.

From where he stood he could see the pale strip of road that wound into the hills to his left. In a few moments the mud wagon would come along and stop here to change horses. It was a special run, supposedly secret, but he'd gotten word that it would be ambushed at Ashford's Station. An hour ago he had gotten Ashford and his wife away, along with their two wranglers; they were safe back in a draw, waiting.

As chief of security for the Toland Mining Company, Morgan paid well for bits of information and had already foiled several robberies because of it. The Toland mines hauled a fortune in gold every year, from the mines to the railroad forty miles away, every delivery well guarded. This one tonight was an exception. But somewhere along the line, someone had talked.

That in itself was a problem, to be taken up later. Right now, he had to make sure the gold got through. Ashford's Station was only a mile or so from the low hills, close to a creek, an ideal location but lonely. The undulating prairie stretched away on three sides, silent now but for the far-off bark of a fox.

Morgan holstered the pistol and levered a shell into the Winchester. His four men were hugging the ground just outside the roadway where the wagon would halt by the corral. One man, Billy North, was inside the near shack. At his signal Billy would toss a match into the kerosene-soaked straw in front of the shack. It ought to give them plenty of light to shoot by.

He tapped his finger on the stock of the rifle. Everything was ready. According to the information he'd received there were three men who would come after the gold. Morgan thought they would probably follow the wagon into the yard, herd the driver and guard into the house, pile the gold into a buckboard and take off. Gold was heavy as hell, they'd need a wagon to haul it. Of course they might just change horses on the mud wagon and take that. But he doubted it. The mud wagon was painted red with the Toland name in big letters on three sides. Everyone in the territory knew it by sight. They'd be stupid to take it.

The wagon was coming. In the still night he could hear the distant hoofbeats and in another few moments could hear the sounds of iron-shod wheels on the rutted road. He could hear the wagon long before he could see it—then it came out of the gloom, a dark, moving silhouette, and rattled into the yard with the driver talking to his teams, hauling back on the brake. As the wagon halted, the driver jumped down and ducked into the corral to take cover as he'd been ordered.

In the next moment two horsemen appeared and Morgan could hear the sounds of another wagon approaching. He gave a long whistle.

Almost instantly fire blazed up from the large patch of straw, flames reaching as high as the shack roof—illuminating two men on horseback. One of them shouted something. A pistol fired, then a fusillade swept both men from the saddles as a buckboard came into the yard and swerved as the driver hauled on the reins, trying to get out of the yard again. The light wagon tipped and went over, spilling the man into the fire. He rolled out and tried to run and was cut down at once.

Then everything was quiet except for the still-crackling flames. Morgan walked into the circle of light. A good night's work. His information had been correct.

Toland, a town named after the mines, was a tiny place that nestled along the folds of a hill several miles from the mines. The same creek that watered the Ashford Station wandered by the town and widened into a pond just outside it.

Old John Toland, who owned the mines, had made plans for bringing the railroad across the prairie from Brinker, forty miles distant; but when he died his son had laid the plans aside as too expensive. The mines, with three major holes, employed some four hundred men, mostly men without wives. The town, therefore, had five bawdy houses, nine saloons, two with dancehalls attached, and only one general store.

There was also one general practitioner and an undertaker. The latter was often busier than the doctor. The undertaker, a lean, almost skinny man with mournful eyes, was named Karl Sawyer. He always wore black in public, was unmarried and usually drank half a bottle of whiskey a day in one of the saloons, allowing his assistant to do most of the work. Sawyer liked to handle the money and drive his elegant black glass-sided hearse.

He and his assistant had just returned from Ashford's, hauling the three bodies that had been gunned down in the attempted robbery. He had laid them out in his workroom for the sheriff to view.

Sheriff Tom Linkhorn had identified two as being on his wanted lists. One of them was worth a hundred dollars. The third was Keno Willis, brother of Frank Willis, the notorious bandit and killer. The sheriff had known Keno personally, a tin-horn gambler and general no-good.

Linkhorn stood outside the undertaker's shop with Shelter Morgan and Sawyer. He would have the local photographer make tintypes of the three, he said, to satisfy the authorities at the county seat that they were indeed gone to their Maker . . . along with Mr. Sawyer's signature on a piece of paper.

"Then you can dig a hole some'eres, Karl, and

kick 'em in."

Sawyer asked, "You ain't going to tell me t'wait for the reward money t'bury 'em is you?"

"The mine will pay to bury them," Morgan said. He smiled at the sheriff. "Then you can send us some of the reward money."

"All right," Linkhorn agreed. "Buy youall a drink?" He looked at the man in black. "You too, Karl."

Karl glanced at the sky. "Early f'me yet, Sheriff. But thanks anyways." he went into the office.

They walked to the nearest saloon and Linkhorn said, "It'll be in the papers you killed Keno Willis. You best watch yore backtrail."

Morgan nodded. "I will. You ever see Frank Willis?"

Linkhorn shook his head. "I knew Keno, a ratty little sonofabitch, but I got a pitcher of Frank in the office."

"I'd like to see it."

"Come on across the street."

They walked across and Linkhorn unlocked his desk and took out a sheaf of posters. He shuffled through them and pulled out one. "This here's him."

Morgan looked at the faded photograph of a man in his 30s, black hair, brows straight across under a low forehead, a knife-sharp mouth and prominent cheekbones.

Linkhorn said, "That was taken in a jail someplace, about five years ago. He could be changed a little bit now."

According to the poster, Willis had been hip-shot at some time in the past and walked with a slight

9

limp. He was wanted for murder and considered very dangerous.

"But he don't know what *you* look like," the sheriff said. "Don't get your pitcher taken."

"Good advice," Shelter said.

It was when he was walking back to his horse that the man with the telegram met him. "You Mr. Morgan, sir?"

"I'm Morgan."

"This here wire's f'you." He handed Morgan a yellow envelope.

Morgan tore it open and read the few words. "Meet you in Claybank on the fifteenth." It was signed: Pomfret.

Morgan read it again, but the words hadn't changed. Claybank in two days. Pomfret was Major General Adolph Pomfret, and he, Shelter Morgan, was under orders. He was in fact a colonel in the United States Army—although that was impossible because Morgan had been a captain in the Confederate Army. But Pomfret did impossible things.

Morgan got on the horse and headed for the mine buildings. He had an agreement with Pomfret; he was his own man between assignments. That's why he was here at Toland. He was marking time until Pomfret sent for him again.

And now the message had come. Morgan felt a twinge of excitement. Whatever the assignment was, it would be unique. Pomfret never sent him on a mundane errand. It was certain to be something out of the ordinary.

CHAPTER TWO

He turned over his duties to an assistant and went home to the boarding house to pack his other shirt. He would travel very light. He was a big man, broad shoulders tapering to a slender waist. He had cold blue eyes in a weathered face framed by dark hair. He put on a battered, sweat-stained Stetson and went out to the stable with his Winchester and a cloth sack of food that Mrs. Larson, the boarding-house owner, had put up for him.

Saddling the gray, he tied on the sack and swung up, shoving the rifle into the boot. What the hell did Pomfret have for him this time?

Claybank was across the hills, an easy two days' ride away, even if he took the stage road. But Morgan headed into the hills, ignoring the road, navigating by dead reckoning. He crossed the road twice as it swung around the hills, taking the easiest course through valleys with the telegraph paralleling it. He met no one and came out of the flinty hills with the town sitting placidly in the plain with a charcoal streak of mountain behind it.

He had never been to Claybank before. It was a slightly larger town than Toland, situated on a crossroads with a few farms on the outskirts. There was an army fort nearby—he had never seen it either—but this country was on the edge of civilization. There had been no Indian troubles for a decade, but Indians didn't go by the rules.

He walked the gray into town and got down in front of the only hotel, the Osborne House. A sign proclaimed it as snake-proof. The clerk at the desk inside was a man of sickly complexion. He shook his head at Morgan's question. No, there was nobody named Pomfret registered. "Maybe he's comin' in on the stage."

"When does it get here?"

The clerk pulled out a silver turnip watch and consulted it gravely. "About three hours, I reckon." He put the watch away. "You goin' to sign in?"

Morgan nodded and signed John Smith. He slapped a dollar on the counter as the clerk turned the register and read the name.

"We put you in number nineteen, Mr. Smith." He handed over a key. "You're the third John Smith this week."

"It's a small world," Morgan said and went outside to the horse, led the gray around back to the stable and stripped off the saddle and bridle. He hung the saddle and leather in the stall, rubbed down the gray with some corn husks, took the Winchester and went inside. He left the rifle in the room, asked the clerk to have the stableboy water and feed the gray and went out to the street.

Half a block up he found a sign: Baths 25¢. He had to build a fire under the water and fill the tub himself but it was worth it to luxuriate in the hot bath. The towel the man gave him was skimpy, but Morgan did not complain. He dressed and went out refreshed. A man ought to have a bath every week if he could.

Next to the baths was a saloon and he went through the swinging doors to a gloomy interior, blinking his eyes in the sudden dark. There was a long bar to the left; the rest of the room was filled with tables for gambling. A half dozen men sat here and there and several stood at the bar where a number of lanterns hung from wires. Behind the bar was a sign: Cold Beer.

Shel halted at the bar and dug down for a coin. A barman with white, wispy hair drifted toward him. "What's your pleasure . . . ?"

"I'll have some of that beer."

The bartender nodded and set a bottle in front of him, taking the coin deftly.

"I just got in. Any news?"

The barman shrugged. "Ever'body's talkin' about the President, that's all, I guess."

"What about him?" Morgan took a swig. The beer was cool, not very cold.

"They say he's gonna come out here to the territory."

"What for?"

"I ain't got any idee." The older man smiled. "I ain't rightly talked to a President in mebbe ten year."

Shel chuckled. "Me neither."

The bartender drifted away down the bar and

Morgan sipped the beer. Who the hell was President now, Grant or Hayes? It was probably Hayes; hadn't he read it somewhere? Presidents didn't mean much out in the sticks. They were almost legendary figures, people that one heard about but never saw.

A woman's voice said, "Youall going to buy me a drink, honey?"

Morgan turned. A woman in pink stood there, smiling at him. She wore a very low-necked dress with ruffles on it and her bare breasts pushed and struggled to get out, barely covered so the nipples made little tents.

She said, "My name's Mandy. What's yours?"

"John Smith."

She laughed. "Of course it is." She was wearing rouge and powder; he could smell the perfume. Over her shoulder he noticed the stairs leading to the second floor. So she probably had a room up there where she took her customers.

He was about to tell her he was not interested when a man grabbed her from behind and swung her around. Goddammit, Mandy, I tole you, git yore ass upstairs!"

She yanked her arm away. "I'm not going! I told you I—"

The man slapped her hard, knocking her into Morgan. Blood gushed from her cut mouth. She would have fallen had he not held her up. The man was shabbily dressed, a stone-brown face and smelled of liquor. Morgan felt annoyed. He shoved his hand into the other's face, the heel of the palm slammed the man back; he lost his balance and sprawled onto the floor.

The woman let out a cry and ran off. Morgan stepped close and the man growled at him, "I gon' kill you fer that—." He yanked out his pistol and Morgan kicked it away. It skittered under the tables and bumped the far wall.

Morgan glanced at the others in the room. "Anybody here know this woman beater?"

No one answered; several smiled and someone said, "Kick his ass out into the street."

Morgan nodded. "Get up," he said to the man, "and get out."

The other scrambled to his feet, ducking away from Morgan. "I be back, mister . . ." He hurried through the swinging doors.

The bartender spoke at Morgan's elbow. "His name's Jed Glover. He a sometime stage driver."

Morgan turned and took up the beer bottle. It was nearly empty. "Where's a good place to eat?"

"Try Maggie's." The barman jerked his thumb. "Down t'end of the street. Ask for her cornbread." He wiped the bar. "You want 'nother beer?"

Shel Morgan left the saloon a half hour later. But instead of going out the street door, he went out the back way, around the block of buildings and approached the front of the saloon on the opposite side of the dark street.

He had a feeling Jed Glover would be waiting from him, and he was right. The man was standing in a doorway with a rifle. A man with a rifle on his shoulder was not unusual in the town and he attracted no notice. Morgan slid into the doorway with the Colt pistol in his hand. Glover must have seen something out of the corner of his eye. He swung the rifle viciously. Morgan ducked under it and laid the pistol barrel along the other's jaw. Glover collapsed in a heap.

"You a pile of trouble, friend," he said aloud and took the rifle to drop in a horse trough as he went back to the hotel.

The westbound stage was only an hour late, and General Pomfret was on board. He was a tall, well dressed man who did not appear tired, as the other passengers did, but nodded to Morgan as he stepped down, gallantly lifting his hat to a woman passenger. He retrieved his bag from a handler and walked to the hotel with Morgan, as they discussed the weather.

Pomfret signed for a room, using the name James Howe, and they went upstairs, locking the room door behind them. Then Pomfret said, "Good to see you, Shel. You're looking fit."

"So are you, General."

They drew chairs closer together and sat. Pomfret said, "I expect you've heard, the President is coming west . . . ?"

"Yes, I heard some gossip."

"It's not gossip. It's the truth. He's making a swing through the territory and we can't talk him out of it."

"Why would you want to?"

"Because he could get himself assassinated." Pomfret patted his pockets for a cigar.

"Assassinated?"

"Yes. There's a very good chance of it." He found

the cigar and bit off the end. "That's why you're here . . . in case you're wondering."

"You expect me to protect the President?" Morgan was astonished.

"No, I don't. But I expect you to grab the man who might do it."

"You know who he is?"

Pomfret nodded. "We think we know who it is. We've got a very goddamned good idea who it is." He struck a match and lighted the cigar, puffing blue smoke. "Let me give you some background. Since the war a flock of secret societies have sprung up — you've probably heard of some of them. They're like weeds all over the country, each one with its own axe to grind." Pomfret waved the cigar. "They come and go and most of 'em do little real harm. But now and then one comes along that could give us headaches."

"And one has . . ."

"Yes. And what's worse, it's largely composed of Copperheads."

Morgan smiled. "They were your problem in the war, not ours."

Pomfret smiled grimly, nodding. "They were Northern Democrats who opposed the war policy and tried to get a negotiated peace. A lot of people called them traitors. We thought they'd died out, but they haven't."

"But the war's over. What do they want now?"

"It seems like they just want to stir up trouble. My opinion is — for what it's worth — that they want to create chaos and grab power . . . maybe put their own man in as President."

Shel Morgan whistled. "Could that be possible?"

"Depending on how many people in high places go along with them. We're just now uncovering the movement." He puffed the cigar. "Others are working that end of it. I'm here to keep the President alive. Let me give you some more background. The leader of this bunch is a man named Wake Bowers. He's a fanatic of the worst kind. And he has a son who is worse, a known killer and an enforcer. He and his band keep the movement in line. The father sets the course and the son sees that everyone stays on it."

"What's the son's name?"

"Gavin Bowers." Pomfret got up and opened his bag. He fished in it and brought out an envelope. "I've got a drawing of him here." He pulled out some papers, frowned at them and handed one to Morgan. "That's him as of last year."

Morgan studied a drawing of a man in his 30s, dark and frowning, an ordinary looking face except for the mouth. He pointed to it. "What's that?"

"His lower lip was badly cut in a fight. It healed up so it looks to be in two parts. Hard to miss. There's no photograph of him, but this is his father, Wake Bowers." He handed Shel a tintype. "However, you won't see Wake out here. He stays in the east." He took the tintype back and slipped it into the envelope.

Morgan set the drawing on the table near them and continued to study it. "So Gavin Bowers is following the President?"

"We think he is, yes."

"Why do you think so? Have you seen him?"

"No, but we have reason to believe — let me tell you a little more. We have been able to get one of our undercover agents into one of their meetings . . . in which Gavin swore to kill the President. Of course in Washington the President is so well guarded that no one could get within half a mile of him. Since Mr. Lincoln's assassination we take enormous precautions as you can imagine."

"But out here in the west is another thing."

"Exactly." Pomfret pointed the cigar. "That's why I called for you."

"You want me to bring Gavin Bowers in."

Pomfret smiled. "You were always a quick study. That's exactly what I want. I want him dead or alive. And my personal preference is to see him with his arms crossed, holding a lily. Do I make myself clear?"

"Yes sir, very clear," Morgan said, smiling.

"Do you have any problems with the idea of protecting a Yankee President?"

Shel looked surprised. "I'm an American!"

"All right. I had to ask."

"What about helpers? Does Bowers have a gang?"

Pomfret shrugged. "I can't help you there. He probably has a couple of henchmen . . ." He stubbed out the cigar. "Is there a restaurant in this town?"

Morgan rose. "Yes. Let's go over to Maggie's."

CHAPTER THREE

The stage had brought in a packet of weeklies and Morgan bought one on the way to the restaurant. Maggie's place was not crowded, a large square room, very warm, smelling of cooked beef and tobacco. They took a table in a corner and Morgan opened the newspaper. On the front page was a story about the President and his party arriving in St. Louis to begin a journey into the wild west.

"Well," Morgan commented, "Everyone in the world knows about it now."

"Impossible to keep a thing like that secret. Any President makes news wherever he goes. Hell, people fall all over themselves to find out what he had for breakfast."

"Why do they want to know?"

General Pomfret shrugged. "Don't ask me. I don't care what he eats."

"How many are traveling with him?"

"Probably about fifty, outside of his immediate family. There's secretaries, at least one cabinet officer, some senators and a flock of reporters and sketch artists. To say nothing of his guards, both uniformed and plainclothes."

"I guess you're keeping his route secret?"

"Impossible to do that either. People want to see and hear him. He makes speeches a couple of times a day . . ." Pomfret frowned at a menu card. "We circulate the guards among the crowds of course."

They ate beef and potatoes, finished with coffee and cigars and walked back to the hotel in the dark. The presidential party would take a steamer from St. Louis, Pomfret said, and go up the Missouri to Kansas City. The real western tour would start from there.

He had letters to write and thought he would turn in early, so Morgan left him. Feeling restless, he walked to the nearest saloon, the Silver Slipper. It had a dancehall attached and he wandered in and watched a stage show. Several young woman were dancing and singing to an enthusiastic crowd. And at the end of the number several men fired revolvers at the ceiling—which was already peppered with holes.

Morgan went back to the bar and ordered beer. The saloon was not crowded, not like, he supposed, it would be on a Saturday night. A dozen men were playing cards at the tables, a few at the faro table and a few hanging around the piano player, suggesting songs. One man danced with a blond girl and several other girls wandered from table to table exchanging banter, giving as good as they took.

One of them was Mandy, the girl he'd seen before. When she noticed him, she came to the bar smiling.

"I didn't thank you for saving me earlier . . ."

"My pleasure. You want a beer?"

"I'd rather have coffee." She motioned to one of the two barmen. "Cup of coffee, Max?"

"Comin' up . . ."

She said, "I thought you were just passing through."

"I am. Staying overnight is all." She was a good looking woman. There was a tiny cut mark at the corner of her mouth where the man had struck her but she hadn't lost any teeth.

The bartender set a coffee mug on the bar and she sipped it, glancing up at him in a provocative way. Drinking his beer, Morgan watched her with rising interest. He hadn't had a woman in a month or more, and where was it carved in stone that he had to go celibate forever?

She moved a little closer so he could smell her perfume and enjoy the way her dress fitted tightly over her ample breasts. She said, "My room is upstairs, number four." Her voice was soft and caressing.

He glanced toward the end of the room. "Up that stairway?"

She nodded. "Or you can go out and come up the outside stairs. They're more private."

"Number four . . . ?"

She smiled. "Why don't I meet you there in a few minutes?"

He finished the beer. "All right. I'll go around."

She moved away and he turned toward the door, smiling inwardly. His ingrained sense of caution did not want him to go up the inner stairway, even though he was a stranger in the town. He had trained himself for so many years to take no chances . . .

He strode out to the dark street and paused, looking about. The stairway must be to his left. He could hear the tinkling music of a piano across the street, a dog was barking behind the buildings, and near him a horse sneezed at a hitchrack. He walked to the end of the building, glanced around and went up. There was an open door at the top; he went through and found himself in a hallway. There were several doors and number four was next to last.

He opened the door and looked in. Mandy was sitting on a bunk bed, entirely naked. She grinned at him. "Come in . . . John Smith."

He chuckled. "That's a pretty outfit."

She shook her tits at him. "Do you like it?"

"Very nice." It was a tiny room, the bunk bed and one chair. A metal mirror screwed to the wall and several pegs for clothes. Not much.

He sat in the chair and pulled at his boots; the music from the saloon below filtered up to them faintly. He put the boots by the chair, pulled the shirt off over his head and pushed off his jeans, folding the pistol and cartridge belt, dropping them by the boots. He laughed as she said, "Mmmmm, you don't even smell bad."

"I just had a bath." He lay beside her on the bunk, sliding his arm under her blond head. Both her hands dived into his crotch and she captured his shaft, snuggling closer, sliding her knee over his hip.

She was soft as a kitten and purred like one. Her voice was a small breath of sound,

"Roll me onto my back . . ."

He did as she said and could contain himself no longer. Reaching, he guided it and she lifted her knees, whispering something so softly he could not hear it. Her face was a pale oval against the blanket, then her arms tightened about him as he pushed deep . . . and warm.

The bunk made small squeaking protests as he moved. Her hands played over his broad back, down to slap his butt, and back again. Time flowed past, bearing them both like leaves on a river, whirling them into another space . . . How long they lay there, he could not have said.

But he came awake, hearing the shuffling sounds of boots in the hallway. Someone was trying to walk silently.

Then he heard the unmistakable sound of a pistol hammer being drawn, click clack. Morgan rolled off the girl and grabbed for the Colt by the chair. The door opened and someone shouted—then a pistol blasted, a terrible roar in the confined space. Morgan's hand closed around the Colt and he fired three times at the huge dark figure in the doorway.

He was conscious of a second shot and of Mandy's screaming.

The figure was gone, sprawling in the hallway, his gun thudding on the boards. It was suddenly still.

Morgan got to his knees beside the bed. "Are you all right?"

"Y-yes—" she answered. "A-are you?"

There was a strong smell of liquor in the hall. "Yes." Morgan stood and pulled on his pants. The man had probably been drunk. Someone was yelling downstairs. They'd be up in a minute.

"Get dressed," he told her. He buckled on the pistol and pulled the shirt over his head, tucking it into the jeans. Men were running up the steps.

Mandy said, "There's a lantern here—"

He struck a match and lifted the lamp chimney, lighting the wick. A half dozen men came along the hallway as he stepped out and held the lantern over the figure on the floor.

It was the man, Jed Glover, his chest smashed to pulp.

Other lanterns were quickly brought and a deputy sheriff arrived, a lean old-timer with a star badge pinned to a low slung cartridge belt. He glanced around the circle of men. "Who done the shootin'?"

Someone pointed to Morgan and he said, "I did."

The deputy knelt by the body, examining it for signs of life. It took only a moment, then he rose again. "He dead all right." He took Morgan aside. "Tell me."

"I had a run-in with him earlier," Morgan said, "down in the saloon. He waited for me across the street and I had to take a rifle away from him. It looks like he followed me up here."

The deputy nodded. "It was dark. How'd you know it was him?"

"I didn't. I was on the bunk with the girl and he slammed the door open and took a shot—if he hadn't been drunk he wouldn't have missed."

The deputy nodded again. "All right. You wait here." He went down the hallway and entered Mandy's room.

He was in the room several minutes. When he

came out he sent someone for the undertaker and came down the hall to Morgan. He hooked both thumbs in his belt. "The girl 'grees with your story." He glanced toward the body. "This feller's name was Jed Glover. I figger a case of jealousy."

"Yes, I think so."

"And a little revenge tossed in. Mandy says you knocked him down in front of witnesses."

"Wasn't much else I could do . . . except shoot him."

"He was a troublemaker. What's yore name?"

"I'm registered at the hotel as John Smith."

"Ummm." The deputy nodded. "You stayin' in town?"

"I'll be leaving in the morning. If it's all right with you."

"That'll be fine, Mr. Smith."

General Pomfret was very annoyed. "You shot somebody?"

"It couldn't be helped. He came looking for trouble—and found it."

"I swear, Shel—everywhere you go—" He shook his head. "You know you've called attention to yourself."

"We're leaving in the morning, aren't we?"

"Yes. We'll head for Kansas City."

Shel went to the door, then came back. "What're you doing out here in the sticks? Why didn't you tell me t'meet you in Kansas City?"

Pomfret smiled innocently. "Because I had other business, Mr. Morgan. Did you think I concerned myself only with you? I actually have other affairs to look after."

"Oh." Morgan made a face. "Of course." He went to the door, glanced back and went out. He should have thought of that. Pomfret was a sly one ...

He returned to Maggie's Restaurant in the morning with Pomfret. They had eggs, bacon and some of Maggie's touted cornbread. It was excellent.

When the eastbound stage arrived they had their bags put aboard and left with it well before midday. Morgan noticed the deputy standing in a doorway, watching. Town marshals were always glad to see gungslingers leave.

It was twenty miles to the next station and they were there in about five hours, tired and dusty. The wranglers changed horses and they went on to the town, another three hour journey.

It was a small burg, called Caprock, and they reached it at dusk. They would stay there overnight. As they got down from the stagecoach, stretching, a boy came through the yard with an armful of papers and Pomfret bought one: the *Caprock Journal,* a weekly. On the first inside page was a picture of Shelter Morgan.

CHAPTER FOUR

Pomfret was very annoyed on seeing it. "Where the devil did they dig that up from!?"

It was a daguerreotype made while Morgan was still in uniform during the war. A group picture, the newspaper had cut out Morgan's likeness and titled it: *Shelter Morgan, well known gunslick*.

The item accompanying it was an account of the shooting of Jed Glover in a house of ill repute. "Morgan entered the cribhouse," according to the story, "and shot down Glover in a fit of jealousy. Morgan and Glover had been embroiled in an altercation earlier in the day and this shooting ended it. The girl was unharmed."

Morgan read the paper, shaking his head. "They've got it all ass-backwards," he said in disgust. "Glover came to the room looking for me."

"Well, it's very bad news, no matter which way they tell it."

Morgan examined the picture from several angles.

"It's about eight years old . . ."

"Yes, but it still looks too much like you." Pomfret chewed a cigar savagely. "They must have had it in their files, for whatever reason . . ." He sighed deeply. "Well, let's hope no one sees it. I imagine that paper has a circulation of no more than a thousand."

"Yes, probably."

There was a weather-beaten hotel near the stage station, advertising beds for travelers. It was a venerable edifice, painted brown with gray trim and they went into the narrow office, signed the register and went upstairs to wash.

Across the street was a restaurant. They got a table and Pomfret spread out a map printed in Washington, D.C. With a black pencil he drew a line from Caprock to Kansas City.

"At this rate it'll take us a week to get there. According to the schedule, the President's party arrives there in eight or nine days."

"Then we'll be there in time."

Pomfret nodded, sighing. "Yes, I suppose so." He folded up the map and tucked it away. "I shouldn't be out here in the sticks at all. I ought to have sense enough to stay at my desk instead of fighting to keep you out of trouble."

Morgan smiled. "Give up. It's a hopeless battle."

The general sighed deeply. "I'm beginning to think you're right."

A search of Keno Willis' effects turned up a letter from his brother, Frank. Frank's return address was a saloon, the Alamo, in Wind River. A letter of particulars, telling about Keno's death along with a newspaper clipping, went to him there.

Frank Willis received the letter in due time, concluded his affairs and saddled up to ride to Toland. Frank was uninterested in the fact that his brother had been killed in the commission of a robbery. Shelter Morgan had gunned Keno down and must pay for it. He vowed to himself to even the score.

When he got to Toland he found that Morgan was no longer there. He had left to go north. No one could tell him why or where Morgan was bound, but Willis headed out, looking for signs.

When he read that Jeb Glover had been killed in a gunfight with a 'John Smith', he asked questions. The description of the killer matched what he knew of Morgan . . . he had never seen Morgan.

When he came at last to Caprock, he was a week behind Morgan.

But then he read the newspaper and smiled, seeing Morgan's picture. Now he knew exactly who he was looking for.

After leaving Caprock, two days later, they came to Kingston, a division point on the railroad. Kingston was a large town, almost a city; it had three hotels and twenty saloons, some of them little more than deadfalls. They put up at the Bemis Hotel, a block from the depot, and had supper in the spacious dining room.

Pomfret got out his map again and studied it as they drank their coffee. The railroad would take them into Kansas City without switching cars. It would be a welcome change from the rattling, dusty stagecoach, that threatened, Pomfret said, to jolt his liver out.

After supper Pomfret went to send some telegrams and Morgan walked along the street stopping in front of an establishment that proclaimed itself an "Entertainment Emporium."

Enthusiastic music came from within, so Morgan opened the door and stepped inside. It was a saloon with a large stage to one side on which a flock of brightly clad girls were dancing. Men were applauding, calling suggestions to the girls and laughing loudly.

It was a huge gaily decorated room, with colored Chinese lanterns hanging from the ceiling and a long, gilded bar with a series of large mirrors before which were stacked glittering piles of glassware. He could see five bartenders, each with white shirts and red vests and there were a dozen or more painted ladies moving among the men.

He went to the bar and ordered beer, and when it came it was cold. They actually had ice! He drank thirstily, feeling back in civilization. Things *were* looking up; he had had two baths in the last week also!

Then the kid showed up. He looked young, probably no older than twenty. He wore a fringed buckskin shirt and a pistol in a black holster hanging from a hand-tooled belt. The holster was tied down. He said, "You're Shelter Morgan." He stood five or six feet away. "I seen you in Toland."

Morgan glanced at him, a youngster with a triangular face and thick black hair. He looked like a dandy.

The kid said, "I'm talkin' to you."

Morgan eyed him. A kid on the prod? "What is it you want?"

"You're a big man in Toland, ain't you? But you're not there now."

"You figured that out, did you?"

The other's voice was suddenly sharp, almost snarling and Morgan realized he was raging, anger eating him up. The kid said, "You pushed me around in Toland but now it's different!"

"I never saw you before."

"You're a liar!"

The room had gradually become quiet. Morgan saw men moving away from behind him and the kid, out of the line of fire. He was holding a large glass stein half filled with beer. He threw it suddenly and the beer drenched the kid's shirt, the heavy glass thumped his chest. The kid pulled his revolver and Morgan's toe lifted it up as it fired. It banged on the bartop and dropped on the far side. Instantly Morgan stepped close and his fist knocked the kid to the floor.

Two bouncers rushed in and grabbed the kid who screamed obscenities as they hustled him to the door and tossed him into the street.

Suddenly everyone was talking again. The music, which had stopped, took up where it had left off. Solemnly a bartender set another glass of beer in front of Morgan.

"Thanks for not shootin' him," he said.

"You know who he is?"

"Name's Cally or Corry—I think it's Corry. You made an enemy, you know."

Morgan smiled. "I think we were enemies before." He sipped the beer.

"Maybe it's your reputation. You know how young guys are."

Morgan sighed. How many enemies could a man have? Well, with Jed Glover gone, it was one less. He smiled ruefully to himself. General Pomfret would have something to say if he learned about the incident. He'd best not tell him—even though it was none of his doing. He wasn't invisible, after all.

He finished the beer, nodded to the barman and toured the room, watching the poker players, eyeing the women. Nearly everyone gave him a glad eye and several slipped their hands into his. One had an interesting suggestion, but he shook his head. He stood by one of the faro tables for a few moments; the cards were running for the house.

When he went out to the street it was with a group of men; he saw no one on the street and went to the hotel without incident. He hoped the kid would think better of whatever he had in mind. Morgan shook his head as he mounted the stairs to his room. He certainly did not want to kill the youngster. What glory in that?

They had breakfast in the morning at a restaurant near the depot and Pomfret kept pulling out his silver mounted watch to consult it. The train was due at 9:45, according to the schedule.

When they finished eating there was still two hours to wait. Their bags were on the loading dock and Pomfret walked up and down the platform trailing cigar smoke.

Morgan sat out of the sun, sitting in a titled-back chair facing the tracks.

The first shot smashed the window near his head. The report was flat and vicious in the still morning air. The second shot shattered the chairback where Morgan had been a second before. He sprawled full length on the platform, the Colt pushed out in front of him, thumbing back the hammer. The kid ran toward the platform, ducking and weaving, firing a pistol in each hand.

Morgan fired twice, hearing Pomfret yell. He missed the kid with the first shot and spun him half around with the second.

The kid's pistols barked and tiles shattered at the eaves and scattered along the platform like huge red hailstones. Another window smashed and a woman screamed inside the waiting room. Morgan's third shot sent the kid down, legs kicking.

For a moment no one spoke, then the station master came flying from his office, yelling at someone to run for the goddamn law! Morgan got up warily — but the kid stayed down.

Pomfret growled, "What the hell was that about?"

Ignoring him, Morgan jumped down and strode across the tracks to stand over the body. The kid was as dead as he would ever be, a bullet through his arm and one through his forehead. With a great sigh, Morgan holstered the Colt. Stupid kid.

Pomfret came up behind him, looking down at the thing that had been a man. Morgan glanced at him. "The kid challenged me last night. I stopped him from fighting and he tried to bushwhack me.'

"You're trouble, Shel. Just plain trouble."

"But I'm the one who's alive."

Pomfret grunted. "That's why we employ you." He turned. "Hellsfire. Now I've got to go smooth things with the goddamn law."

CHAPTER FIVE

Shel Morgan was astonished at how adroitly General Pomfret handled the local law. The county sheriff was called, riding to the scene, having heard some of the facts. He glowered at Morgan and at the body in the weeds across the tracks. But then Pomfret took him aside and talked for half an hour. The two walked up and down the platform alone and the sheriff began to nod.

He did not speak to Morgan at all. Men came and took the body away in a wagon; the sheriff and Pomfret shook hands and the lawman rode away.

Morgan said, "I was sure I'd spend some time in the hoosegow."

"You would have if I didn't work directly under the President."

"Can the President shoot people and get away with it?"

Pomfret turned a bland face to him. "Certainly, while he's in office." He did not add, and so can I, but the inference was plain, Morgan thought.

The train arrived almost on schedule and they got aboard. There were four passenger cars, a baggage car and a caboose. They took seats at the rear of the first car; they were plum colored and hard, the windows were grimy but it was warm enough in the car so the wood stove at the end of the aisle was not needed.

Pomfret opened the newspaper he'd bought in the station; Morgan tipped his battered hat over his face and tried to sleep. But he kept seeing the kid running at him across the lot with two guns firing. The kid had said that Morgan had pushed him around in Toland—done something to him, he was not definite. Maybe he'd applied for a job as a guard and been turned down for one reason or another. Morgan could think of nothing else; he himself had certainly never seen the kid before in his life. But he'd been the chief security officer at the mine . . .

Pomfret finished with the paper and put it aside, looking sidelong at Morgan. "We've got to get you some decent clothes when we get to Kansas City. You can't go about like that."

Morgan lifted the hat and looked at him. "Like what?"

"Look at you, dirty jeans and a gunbelt. Civilized people will think you're a desperado. The police will lock you up."

Morgan grinned at him. "You won't let them."

"And that hat! It's a disaster. It badly needs throwing away."

Morgan frowned at it. "It's a good hat. It's got years of wear in it."

Pomfret sighed deeply. "You're trouble, and you're impossible."

"And you can't get along without me."

Pomfret rolled his eyes. "Unfortunately."

An hour before midday the train stopped at a tiny cluster of houses and a spur line. With much chugging and puffing a dining car was added just in front of the baggage car and, seeing it, Pomfret's spirits rose.

"Our first real touch of civilization. I wonder if they also have a bar?"

An older man in a white coat came through the cars with menu cards. Those who wished to eat in the diner were given the cards and a seating number. Many people had brought food with them, and some bought food from a candy butcher who came through hawking his wares.

But Pomfret insisted they go into the diner. "The taxpayers of the United States want you to have a good meal," he said. "Come along."

They were seated at a table with a dazzling white cloth, and in a moment a chunky man with side whiskers, accompanied by a young woman, were seated opposite them.

Pomfret immediately introduced himself, "I'm General Pomfret and this is one of my aides, Colonel Howe."

The chunky man gave them what he undoubtedly thought of as a smile. "I'm Rufus Bates, House of Representatives. This is my daughter, Amanda."

"Charmed," Pomfret said. Morgan smiled at the girl. She was very pretty and seemed quite shy, lowering her eyes at his glance.

When they gave their orders, Pomfret and the politician began talking politics at once and Morgan leaned back, relaxing. He was seated opposite the girl and all at once was conscious that her foot was touching his. In a moment the foot was caught between both of hers and she was pressing . . .

Though her gaze was lowered demurely.

How interesting that was. He examined her more closely. She was about 19, surely no older. Her hair had a tinge of red and her lashes were long and black. She had long, supple hands and her skin looked to be sheer velvet. Now and then she gave him a quick glance and he saw that her eyes were dark and expressive, and her lips had the hint of a smile. She knew exactly what she was doing.

However, when Pomfret directed a question to her, she had to ask him to repeat it. "I'm sorry, sir, I was thinking of—of something else."

So was he, Morgan thought. Something that couldn't be done on a train like this.

He did not get a chance to talk with her alone for another hour. When they finished eating the two men continued their conversation with cigars and Morgan followed Amanda into the passenger car and sat by her.

When they were seated, side by side, her first question startled him. "How many men have you killed?"

"Why do you want to know?"

"But you have, haven't you?" Her face was eager.

"Well, yes, in the war . . ."

"No, no, not in the war!" She indicated the Colt pistol by his side. "I mean with that."

"What if I said none?"

She let her breath out as if annoyed. "I know who you are."

"What?"

"You're Shelter Morgan. General Pomfret said your name was Howe, but it's not. I've seen your picture."

He smiled ruefully. That damned picture again. Maybe he had better grow a beard . . . or wear a mask. He said, "Please don't tell anyone."

"Are you on a secret mission?"

He hesitated, unused to interrogations from pretty young women — who apparently had amorous intentions. "I would rather not be known."

She nodded as if she understood. "You have enemies . . . ?"

"Yes, a few."

She put her hand out and touched the Colt revolver as if it were a precious jewel. "How many men have you killed?"

"A few," he admitted.

She glanced up at him, then lowered her eyes demurely. "Would you like to go to bed with me?"

He took a quick breath. Girls of her station didn't ask that kind of question. It took his breath away. He tried to think of a reasonable answer and was saved at the last minute by her father. He came along the aisle and stopped by them.

"Come, Amanda." He gave Morgan another cold smile and turned away. Amanda looked after him with a frown furrowing her smooth forehead, then she rose slowly.

"I have to go . . ."

Morgan nodded and rose slightly. She said, "I'll see you again?"

"Of course," he said quickly, and watched her

back as she followed her father into the next car.

Jesus! What kind of a girl was she? She turned at the door and gave him a smile and was gone. He sank back on the hard seat, staring out the window, seeing nothing. He had heard, vaguely, about aggressive women—not whores—but had never met one. Was Amanda one of them? He was surprised now that she hadn't grabbed his cock instead of the pistol.

Pomfret came and plopped down beside him. "Dull man, that congressman. But she was a pretty little thing, wasn't she?"

"Oh yes. Pretty as hell."

"Must favor her mother. Not a trace of her father in her that I could see. I sincerely hope you didn't say anything out of the way to her."

Morgan looked at him. "What?"

Pomfret shrugged. "Well, you know, you live among rough people. This little girl is refined and sweet and probably doesn't know the meaning of— What's so funny?"

Morgan shook his head. "Nothing."

"Mmmmm." The general pulled out his watch and studied it. "We'll be in Kansas City this time tomorrow. God, I'll be glad of a decent bed and food that doesn't taste like plaster."

"Tell me how the President is guarded."

"His immediate guards are all police-trained. They wear plainclothes and are well armed and go everywhere with him. Some of us have been trying to get Congress to finance a regular service to protect the President, but so far we haven't the votes. In my opinion the guard service we have now is hit and miss. There's too big a turn-over and I think they could be better trained in some instances."

"But it's not easy to get close to him?"

"Well, yes and no. It's impossible to put men all around him when he's in the midst of a gathering. We circulate them in the crowd and get them as close as we can without causing annoyance. Local politicians are forever trying to shake his hand, get their pictures taken with him or be seen talking to him. They think it makes them bigger men back home. Especially if they're of his party. It's a problem. And added to that, the President doesn't want to be hampered. He goes into crowds shaking hands like he's still running for office." Pomfret shook his head. "I wish we could nail him to a board and just wave it at them."

"Have you told me everything about Gavin Bowers?"

"I think so. I asked some of our men how they'd go about assassinating the President if they had to do it. Several said they thought he would be vulnerable to a rifle shot from a distance. What do you think?"

Morgan nodded slowly. "I think so too. It would be a very good idea not to let anyone know in advance where the President was expected to be."

"Yes. We've thought of that. And it's a good idea—except for parades. There's no way we can protect him in a parade—that I can think of. We can put a steel vest on him, but that's about all."

"What about using someone who looks like him?"

Pomfret shook his head. "He'd never stand for it. It was suggested once and he got angry, saying it would be fraud."

Morgan had another chance to see Amanda when they all had supper together in the dining car. But there was no opportunity to speak to her alone. Her father told rambling stories about local politics and the hours passed on leaden feet.

A man named Pullman had invented a sleeping car, but those cars were not yet used on every railroad. Morgan and Pomfret and the other passengers had to make do the time-honored way, sleeping upright in their seats . . . fully dressed.

It was a cut above sleeping on the ground, Morgan thought, but it was definitely not heaven.

Long after Pomfret was asleep, snoring slightly, Morgan walked into the next car and looked at Amanda. She and her father were both asleep and the car was very dark. What if she should waken and see him standing there . . . What question would she ask of him then!

He hurried back to his seat by Pomfret.

CHAPTER SIX

The train was ahead of schedule when it arrived in the Kansas City station. A large depot wagon met the train with the name of the hotel blazoned on it: Cambria House. Pomfret headed for it immediately and as they were seated, Amanda and her father appeared and climbed in with them. The congressman looked at Morgan with less than his usual enthusiasm but Amanda smiled on seeing them and gave Morgan several sly under-the-lashes glances, which even Pomfret noticed.

It was a half mile drive to the hotel, an ornate brick and stone building on a corner. The Cambria was across the street from the Bedford where, Pomfret said, the presidential party would stay. The party had not yet arrived, according to the desk clerk when they registered. Pomfret bought a newspaper, a daily, and took it to their suite.

When they got upstairs in the room he said, "What's between you and that girl, Amanda?"

"Nothing. I've hardly spoken a dozen words to her."

"I saw the way she looked at you."

"And you're blaming me for the way she looks?"

Pomfret sighed deeply and sat in an easy chair. "Very well, Morgan. But you stay away from her. She's a sweet, innocent girl and I don't want you leading her down the garden path—we've got enough troubles as it is."

"Yes, General."

Pomfret grunted.

Early the next morning Pomfret was up and out and did not return to the hotel until just before midday. He had another man with him, a skinny, sallow-faced man with the look of a shoe-clerk, dressed in very ordinary clothes. Pomfret said, "This is Bill Tompkins, one of our best agents. Bill, meet Shelter Morgan."

They shook and Tompkins said, "I've heard a lot about you, Colonel Morgan. Glad you're on our side."

Morgan nodded. So this was what a secret agent looked like. Not very dashing.

Pomfret lighted a cigar and they pulled chairs together. "For your benefit, Shel, there's a company of Wake Bowers' people here in Kansas City."

"Company?"

"That's what they call themselves." Pomfret indicated Tompkins. "Tell him, Bill."

The agent nodded. "I managed to infiltrate the local company. It's headed by a man named Luke Daniels who is a thug like most of them."

"How many are there?"

"The company has probably about forty members all in all. They're composed of thugs as I said, some ex-soldiers too, but all of them have grievances against the Washington government, real or fancied."

Pomfret said, "Bill's grievance is that the government promised him a postmastership when he was discharged from the army, and it never came through."

Bill smiled. "And I've got the forged letters to prove it."

Morgan asked, "What do these people expect to accomplish?"

Bill glanced at Pomfret. "It's a way to grab some power and maybe some wealth. Luke Daniels is a big man in this town now, among certain people. He's got more notoriety as a leader of the Company than he would as an armed robber."

Pomfret said, "There are always people willing to finance or aid such men, though they don't get involved themselves. So for every obvious member of the secret Company, there are probably twenty others supporting them. And as the Company grows, so will the supporters, by leaps and bounds."

"In other words, they're attracting a certain kind of person."

"Absolutely." Pomfret puffed the cigar. "Right now the Company is underground, waiting for the day when they can come out into the light. Then they'll really be dangerous! People will flock to them, not really knowing what they stand for."

Bill said, "They have grandiose plans, such as their own newspaper . . . electing their own people to high office . . . Wake Bowers is a crook and a no-good, but he has brains."

"What about an assassination attempt?" Morgan asked. "Will this Company help Gavin Bowers?"

"Of course. If he asks for help." Bill Tompkins shrugged. "I haven't seen him yet. I'll let the general know the minute I find out." He nodded to Pomfret.

"Where do you meet?"

"Different places. Sometimes outside the city. But there is a central core, called the staff. It's composed of Luke Daniels and four others. They run the organization, make most of the decisions—just like the army."

"I have their names," Pomfret said, "and Daniels' address. He runs a feed store on the far side of town."

"Then why don't you have the police round them all up?"

Pomfret made a face. "On what charge? We know they're conspiring to assassinate the President, but we can't prove a thing. And if we rounded up Daniels and his staff, there's still Gavin Bowers at large, and he'd be warned that we know about the Company. If we could find Bowers I'd jail *him* in a second."

There were a dozen or more reporters with the presidential party and they sent to their respective papers reams of "news" about the traveling chief executive. He had had oatmeal for breakfast, he had taken a stroll about the decks of the steamer with Senator Cobb and the Secretary of the Interior . . .

He had talked with a little girl in the saloon and patted her head. He had . . .

Gavin Bowers, in a following steamer, read everything he could find on the President's journey, especially about the party itself. Who composed the entourage . . . what guards were there and what precautions were taken. Reading every paper he could get his hands on, Bowers gleaned more information than the presidential guards would have liked.

He was traveling as a respectable business man; he had grown a beard to change his appearance, and he was never seen in public without his pipe. The pipestem fitted into the cleft of his lip which made the lip much less noticeable. He kept to himself on the steamer, took his meals in his cabin and was accompanied by two aides, both well dressed and as retiring as himself.

Bowers and his aides made no impression on the other passengers, was remembered by none because he blended in so well, and got off the boat in Kansas City and was met by Luke Daniels with a closed carriage.

The President's arrival caused a huge stir in the city. No other President had ever traveled to Kansas City and every newspaper was filled with incident and human interest and each printed the route of the welcoming parade.

Shel Morgan shook his head over it. "The route is lined with buildings, any one of which could conceal a rifleman."

"What do you suggest?" Pomfret asked.

"Can he ride?"

"He's an excellent horseman."

"Then put him and a half dozen others on spirited horses. Let him move about as much as possible. He'll make a much poorer target."

Pomfret shook his head and said gravely, "It's already been put forth. The President will have none of it. He considers it would be undignified."

"So is a bullet in the heart."

"Nevertheless it's out of the question. Think of something else."

"He'll ride in a carriage then?"

"Yes."

"Then bullet-proof it."

Pomfret smiled and patted his pockets for a cigar. "We already have. What do you think we do all day in Washington?"

"I've often wondered."

"He wanted to ride in an open carriage but we were able to talk him out of that, praise the Lord. So he'll ride with the First Lady and several others in a nice bullet-proof closed carriage and we'll all hope for the best. The damned parade is our biggest worry."

"What about speeches?"

"There are several scheduled. The first one will be at the ball grounds at the end of the parade. It's an open field, no buildings around. No place for a rifleman to hide. We'll have mounted police thick around the field and others in the crowd."

"That's good . . ."

"The second speech will be for the honored

guests, a very elite gathering by invitation only. The building will be searched and searched again. No one can get in without our knowing it."

"No windows?"

"No. No windows to shoot through. There'll be a dinner first at about 9 P.M., then the speech."

"Where will it be held?"

"At the Bedford Hotel where the President is staying. There's an excellent ballroom for the occasion."

"The Bedford Hotel! There must be five hundred people in it now. How are you going to search all the rooms?"

"Oh, for God's sake, we're not going to search the rooms. There's no need for that. We'll search the ballroom and the adjoining rooms and halls and every nook and cranny . . . Uniformed guards will be stationed at every door. The President will be escorted from and to his suite . . ."

Morgan sighed. It sounded all right. Pomfret was on top of the thing. He said, "Now that the big brass has arrived, we have to assume that Gavin Bowers is here too. I want to meet with Bill Tompkins again. It's time I got out into the streets. The papers say the parade starts at ten in the morning."

"Yes." Pomfret lighted the cigar. "It'll be over in less than an hour. When do you want to see Tompkins?"

"Now. Tonight."

"All right. I'll send for him."

"No, let me go to him. We don't want him seen coming here."

"Better yet, I'll send a boy and have Tompkins meet you. The boy will seem to be delivering a paper or something. Why don't you meet at the corner of the park on Sanford Street. There's a fountain there."

"Good idea."

Pomfret got up and went out. He was back in the room in fifteen minutes, nodding. "Give the boy half an hour to get to Tompkins, another half hour for him to get to the fountain . . ." He eyed Morgan. "Don't wear that gun. Have you got a shoulder holster?"

"No. I'll carry it under a coat in my belt."

"Good. But try not to shoot anybody."

"You're spoiling all my fun."

Pomfret sighed at him. He puffed the cigar, seemed about to say something and apparently thought better of it. He found a piece of paper and drew a quick map. "Here's where we are and here's the park. It's only a half mile or less . . ."

"I'll walk it then." Morgan studied the map, went into the next room for a coat and slid the revolver into his belt. The coat hid it well enough. He slipped a half dozen cartridges into the coat pockets and took up his battered hat.

Pomfret looked him over and nodded. "You'll pass in the dark."

Morgan stifled a retort and went out quickly. Pomfret could be pompous . . . It must be his long military service.

The hotel kitchen was closed but the door was unlocked. Morgan tried it and slipped inside when no one was looking in his direction. He went from the kitchen area into a hallway that led to the rear, past the servants lockers and storerooms. The door to the outside was locked, but he unbolted it and went through. If it was unnoticed, he'd come back the same way.

He found himself in a wide alley that was full of trash bins and garbage cans. It led to the sidestreet, deserted at this hour. It was a fifteen minute walk to the park though he did not hurry. A few small carriages and buggies were on the streets and one or two horsemen but no one on foot. He walked through the small park and approached the fountain.

Bill Tompkins came from the opposite direction, smoking a cigar. He motioned and they met in the deep shadow of a row of trees. Tompkins said, "He's here in town."

"Gavin Bowers?"

"Yes. One of our men picked him up at the landing. He came in on a steamboat shortly after the President and his party. We were expecting something of the sort and had the landing well covered."

"You're positive it was Bowers?"

Tompkins smiled, showing the sheen of teeth. "He was met by Luke Daniels. Daniels had a rig waiting. Gavin's got a beard now, but our man is positive it was him. He's seen him many times."

"Were you able to follow him?"

"Oh yes. He was followed to a hotel on the south side of town. It's a small, seedy place, probably controlled by Daniels. We've got men watching it now."

"Damn good work. Where is the hotel?"

"It's called the Cutler House and it's on Dearing Street. I hope you're not thinking of going there." Tompkins gestured with the cigar. "He's got two men with him, probably killers. And Luke may have some of the Company there also. You'd walk into a trap."

"What if I just checked it at the hotel, acted like a wanted man?"

Tompkins shook his head. "I doubt if you'd be any better off for doing it. They'd watch you like a hawk, especially now when things are moving. As I told you, they control the hotel more than likely. Oh — and there's one more thing to tell General Pomfret. They are expecting someone of importance very soon."

"Someone who's coming to town?"

"Yes. Someone in the government. I haven't been able to find out his name. The Company has many supporters who are secret. It may be someone in the President's party."

"I'll tell him. You say Bowers has a beard now?"

"Yes, a beard and a mustache. He looks very respectable and so do his henchmen. He'd be hard to pick out of a crowd."

"That makes him more dangerous."

"It certainly does."

"What about those henchmen — what do they know about them?"

"Nothing yet. But we can assume they know their business. I doubt if Bowers would have brought a couple of dolts with him."

"You mean they may be expert riflemen?"

"Exactly." Tompkins dropped the cigar and

stepped on it. "But the general is a good man and so are the people directly guarding the President. Bowers won't have it that easy."

"It only takes one bullet." Morgan hunched his shoulders as if against the cold. "I wonder how fanatic they are, this Bowers bunch."

"What d'you mean?"

"I mean, are they willing to be killed to get a good shot at the President?"

"I guess we'll find out," Tompkins said.

CHAPTER SEVEN

Morgan did not return directly to the hotel but wandered through the streets where the parade would take place next morning. There were many three-story and some four-story buildings along the route. He could imagine that most of the windows would be filled with onlookers, cheering and throwing torn paper. There might easily be enough noise to drown a rifle shot. And unless one were looking at the spot from which the rifle was fired, the puff of smoke would not be noticed.

On the other hand, it would not be easy to shoot a man inside a roofed carriage, unless he were leaning out, and the President was unlikely to do that.

In that light, the parade might well go off without incident. If Bowers tried and failed—the next time would be very much more difficult. The assassin would probably be highly interested in getting away after his deed was done, and he could expect the area to be immediately surrounded—unless he were a martyr. And good journeyman martyrs were in short supply, in Morgan's experience. Especially if they were also thieves and murderers.

When he got back to the hotel Pomfret was up and reading, puffing smoke from one of his black cigars. "Where the hell have you been?"

"I talked to Bill Tompkins."

"Did you shoot anybody tonight?"

Morgan sat and put his feet up. "Sometimes weeks go by and I don't shoot anybody. Tompkins says Bowers and the Company are expecting someone of importance to show up."

Pomfret grunted.

The parade the next morning went off without a hitch. And despite what Pomfret had said about the President and his wife riding in a closed carriage — it did not happen. Apparently the President exercised his authority, overriding all objections, and rode the entire length of the parade with the First Lady and several others, in an open carriage.

At several places the crowds were enthusiastic, shouting and screaming and men fired shots into the air even though the police and guards did their best to deter them. It was generally a happy crowd and Morgan, prowling the length of it, saw only a few arrests. Barred wagons stood by, ready to haul offenders off to the calaboose.

The night before, Morgan had added a mustache and beard to the drawing of Gavin Bowers, but he saw no one who resembled the sketch.

When the parade was finished the President was

whisked to the ball grounds; the First Lady was taken back to the Bedford, and the President delivered a short speech which was probably heard only by those in the first dozen rows of people. But when he sat down finally everyone cheered, and when the evening papers came out, the affair was called a huge success, and it was announced that in three days the presidential party would move on to Topeka.

On the night of the parade, Morgan met Amanda on the stairs. Her father was away at a meeting, she said, and she was going down to buy a newspaper. "He goes to so many meetings, you know, and leaves me alone."

"Do you always travel with him — what about your mother?"

"She died four years ago. Yes, I usually travel with him. I act as his secretary." She took his arm and they went back downstairs. There was a kiosk in front of the hotel and she bought her paper and they went back inside to sit by a potted plant. She was excited, having seen the President earlier. She had never seen him before though she had lived in Washington several years.

"Father never takes me to functions where he is. Of course father is of the other party and dislikes him very much."

"Then your father isn't here to see the President?"

"No, certainly not. And the President is speaking, probably this very minute, right across the street."

"Yes, I know." Pomfret was there, undoubtedly

pacing the floor . . . Morgan felt her hand slide along his thigh. Her eyes were shining and she leaned toward him. He intercepted her fingers before they reached his crotch and was holding her hand when a stern voice behind them barked, "Amanda!"

She jerked her hand away from him and stiffened.

Morgan turned to look into the red, angry face of Rufus Bates. He smiled, "Hello, Congressman."

Bates ignored him. "Get upstairs at once, Amanda."

"Yes, father," she said demurely. She rose and moved toward the stairway. Bates glared at him and followed.

The street outside the hotel was blue with troops and police. There was even a troop of cavalry moving through the throngs of people, walking their horses. It was impossible to get into the hotel unless one was a guest. Morgan went upstairs to bed.

Pomfret had been up most of the night and was grumpy in the morning. The President, he said, would be staying at the estate of a powerful political backer for the next day or two and would be closely guarded with not even the press allowed to enter the grounds. On the third day he would travel to Topeka.

Morgan met with Bill Tompkins again that evening. They strolled through the park and halted by the fountain. Gavin Bowers was determined to move against the President — or so he said, Tompkins told him, but so far he'd found the President too well guarded.

"He was in an open carriage in the parade."

"Yes, but the newspapers had said he would not be, and then there was no time to prepare. Even an assassin must make his plans." Tompkins rolled a cigar in his fingers. "I won't be able to follow to Topeka. I'm not one of those chosen, and if I go it will arouse much suspicion."

"If you are seen."

"No, it's impossible. They would know. I must go about my regular affairs or someone would come looking for me. I think there is one thing you must do to resolve this situation. General Pomfret would not agree with me . . ."

"What is it?"

"Gavin Bowers must be killed. If he is gone the entire assassination idea would fall apart. Luke Daniels is not smart enough to do it. As I have said, he is only a thug."

"You're telling me to kill Bowers?"

Tompkins shrugged. "If you can manage it. You needn't mention to Pomfret that I suggested it." He put the cigar in his mouth but did not light it. "I must get back."

They shook hands and Tompkins said again, "Bowers is the key." He turned and walked into the dark.

Morgan looked after him, hands thrust into pockets. He was probably right. Assassinate the assassinator. What was it General Bedford Forrest said in the war . . . "git thar fust with the mostest . . ."

He walked to the main avenue and hired a cabby to drive him to Dearing Street. "How far is the Cutler House?"

The cabbie, an older man with a face like that on a worn coin, was surprised. "You want t'go there?"

"How far?"

" 'Bout a mile."

"Take me half way."

The man nodded and clucked at his horse. When he let Morgan off he pointed. "Thataway on the right. It got a big sign over the door."

"Thanks."

The cabby was right; he found the hotel easily, set amid other buildings, a livery stable, a cobbler, a deadfall . . . He stood across the street from it, in the shadow of a closed cafe, and looked it over . . . not a big place. Tompkins had warned him not to go inside; had any of the Company seen him with Pomfret? It was possible. He might go in, never to come out again.

While he weighed the pros and cons a horse came clip clopping along the dirt street, pulling a rented cab. It stopped in front of the hotel and Congressman Rufus Bates got out, glanced around and went inside.

Morgan whistled. Bates must be the important man Bill Tompkins had mentioned! Bates was in on the plot to kill the President!

It was a terrible temptation to go across, enter the building and take his chances and he had almost decided to try it when two men came out and stood by the front door. In a moment they were joined by a third who carried a shotgun. The third man walked to the end of the building and disappeared around the side. The two then went back inside.

Morgan sighed deeply. They had the place well

guarded. He waited for an hour but Bates did not come out again. There was doubtless a stable behind the building and he might have left that way.

Pomfret was astounded when Morgan got back to the hotel and told him about Bates. "The man is a traitor!"

"I didn't actually see him talking with Bowers . . ."

Pomfret eyed him. "Are you a lawyer now? Why else would he have gone there?"

"Is Bates a wealthy man?"

"I have no idea. He is not an important figure in the capitol. You think he's helping the Company with money?"

"Maybe. Amanda told me he hates the President."

"You've been talking to her again?"

"Only for a moment while she was buying a newspaper."

"Ummm."

"What can you do about Bates?"

Pomfret went to a window and stared out. "Not much. He's a United States Congressman, after all. We'd have to catch him red-handed." He turned. "But at least now we know about him. I'll pass it on to the proper authorities. Does Bates strike you as an assassin?"

"He himself? No. He's a grouchy old man."

"But as a Congressman he could walk up to the President and shoot him while they shook hands."

Morgan made a face. "You won't let him do that, will you?"

"It's not my job to guard the President. But I'll pass it on . . . don't let Bates close."

61

The next day Pomfret decided to go to Topeka at once, muttering something about other affairs. Morgan would stay one more day, hoping to learn something about Bowers. He accompanied Pomfret to the railroad station well before midday; Topeka was only a short distance, a few hours at most. He would rejoin the general before nightfall, or the next morning.

He watched the train pull out and walked back through the station, thinking he might well go to see Bill Tompkins at his feed store, to check with him one last time.

There was a row of cabs for hire along the street and he headed that way, noticing a group of horsemen that came up on his left. There were four men, walking their mounts single file, none of them paying any attention to him. None of them looked familiar to Morgan.

But when they came abreast of him, perhaps twenty feet away, the leading rider drew a pistol.

Morgan saw the motion out of the corner of his eye. He turned his head as the horseman extended his arm and fired directly at him!

CHAPTER EIGHT

Morgan stopped short and the bullet cracked past his nose. Beside the walk was a grassy plot. He dived toward it and rolled, pulling the Colt pistol. The horsemen turned toward him as he fired. The leading horseman was swept from the saddle and his shot went into the air.

Morgan rolled again and fired at the second man, hitting the horse. Powder smoke eddied as bullets rapped into the ground near him. Thumbing the hammer, he fired at the third and fourth men, hearing the horse scream. It went down flailing its legs.

The fourth man had also been hit. He swayed from the saddle, firing into the ground. The third horseman galloped by him, shouting. Morgan got to his knees and fired again and again, emptying the pistol. He saw the rider slump, but he stayed on the horse and disappeared.

Getting to his feet, Morgan pushed brass from the cylinder and reloaded as quickly as he could. No one was firing at him. Three men were down and half a hundred people were in the vicinity, all frozen, staring at him, some with mouths open. The downed horse still screamed and Morgan went to him and put a bullet into its brain. The rider lay on his back, apparently knocked unconscious by the hard fall, the horse half atop him. Morgan took his pistol and a knife . . . as the law arrived.

He handed the weapons over and identified himself. The fourth man was dead, staring into the sky with sightless eyes. The first man had a bullet in his side and lay twitching. Morgan had never seen any of them before.

He told the disbelieving police, "They came along here and started firing at me. I think they must have thought I was someone else."

Several in the crowd stated the same thing, that the man was suddenly fired on and had only defended himself. One assailant had gotten away.

The men were taken away, one to the morgue, and Morgan was asked to come along to the station house. The police could not believe he knew none of them. "They are all complete strangers to me!" He had seen a friend off on the train and, as he started back to the hotel, had been suddenly attacked by four horsemen.

The prisoner was questioned; his name was Henry Dobbs. He admitted, after a hour in the basement of the station being worked over, that he and the other three had been hired to kill Morgan. He maintained steadfastly that he did not know why. The man who had made his escape had done the hiring. His name was Tom Deberry, and he was known to the police as an armed robber. The dead man's name was Silas Metzer. Dobbs knew the fourth man only as Frank.

Morgan could not tell them why he had been selected for oblivion; he continued to state he knew none of them and could not imagine why he had been fingered. He did not invoke General Pomfret's name.

A magistrate let Morgan go finally and he returned to the hotel. Did Gavin Bowers know what he looked like? Who had pointed him out? Could it have been Congressman Rufus Bates?

Gavin Bowers was furious when he heard what had happened. The attempt on Shelter Morgan's life had been badly bungled. Tom Deberry had been handsomely paid to gun him down and had made a mess of it. Four guns could not kill Morgan! And they had the advantage of surprise!

Deberry had gotten away with a hole in one arm and had left for parts unknown, not wishing to face Bowers. It was clear that Morgan had been badly underestimated.

There was no point in remaining longer in Kansas City. Morgan packed his few possessions and took the train to Topeka, arriving after dark without further incident. Pomfret had reserved a hotel room for him, only a cubicle—rooms were at a premium since the President was expected the next day and people were flocking to the town to gawk.

Pomfret had heard about the shooting and was annoyed. "Bullets follow you everywhere! It's a wonder you're alive!"

"It's because I'm working for you."

Pomfret eyed him. "You didn't give your right name . . . ?"

"No . . . nor mention you. Where is the President staying?"

"There's only one place in town, the Belmont. It's got a bridal suite they're remodeling to make it a Presidential suite. There'll be a parade when he gets here and some speeches as usual. I doubt if he'll stay more than a day."

Morgan went out to look at the Belmont Hotel. It was a grand edifice—for Topeka. There were other hotels, but as Pomfret said, only one that could house a President. It had four stories and considerable marble in the front. Police were in evidence and there was much bustle; men were putting up banners welcoming the distinguished visitor.

He started at one end of the main street and went into each saloon, showing the drawing of Gavin Bowers, asking, "Have you seen this man?" No one had. He spent three hours at the task, visiting all the saloons in the main part of town. A few barmen lingered over the portrait, then finally shook their heads. They could not be sure. He tried the lesser hotels and a few boarding houses with the same result. Maybe Bowers had shaved off the beard.

When he returned to the hotel Pomfret had left and did not appear till dark. "The President will be here in the morning."

"What's the program?"

"Let's get something to eat, I'm starved." They crossed the street to a restaurant. "The party will be met at the station and the parade will start from there."

"Don't send any open carriages."

Pomfret nodded quickly. "That's a good idea. They won't have time to send for another. We'll make some excuse . . ."

It was a genteel restaurant, with tableclothes and flowers in vases. They were led to a table and Pomfret ordered French wine. "Have you heard anything of Bowers?"

"Nothing." He told Pomfret of his search with the portrait.

"Hmmm. I'm told there is no Company in this town. Probably some adherents but no organized group."

"How long is the President staying?"

"Overnight. He'll make one speech and get out. How many votes are there in this place?" Pomfret consulted the menu. "I believe I'll have the deep fried squab. Why don't you have the *Foie de Veau Menagere?*"

"What the hell is that?"

"Liver.'

"I'll have steak—if they have anything that simple."

When the wine came, Pomfret sipped it, inhaling the bouquet. "Too bad we'll never grow decent grapes in this country. . . ." He sighed. "Well, Americans simply don't care for wine. I guess it's national trait."

"Where did you learn it?"

"I've spent years in Europe—military missions. When in Rome, you know . . ."

They had just finished the meal when the marshal showed up. He stood by their table and Morgan noticed he held a revolver down by his side and showed them a badge.

"A United States Marshal!" Pomfret said in surprise. "What is it?"

The marshal spoke to Morgan. "You're Shelter Morgan?"

Morgan glanced at the general. "Yes . . ."

"You're under arrest, sir. I must ask you to hand over your weapon and come with me."

"What the hell is this!" Pomfret said, his voice rasping. "This man is in the employ of the War Department."

"I'm sorry, sir." He put the badge away. "Your gun, Mr. Morgan."

The marshal was a big man, rawboned and hard looking. His revolver followed the move closely as Morgan drew the Colt and laid it on the table. The marshal slipped it deftly into his belt and motioned Morgan to rise.

"I demand an explanation!" Pomfret said. "What is this about?"

"There was a shooting in Kansas City, sir. Mr. Morgan did not give his right name. A judge has issued a warrant for his arrest."

"But the facts were clear! He only defended himself!"

"I've read the report, sir. Will you come with me, Mr. Morgan." He motioned with the gun.

Morgan got to his feet and Pomfret said, "We'll

see about this, Shel."

Outside the restaurant on the dark street, the marshal motioned and he mounted one of the two horses there and moved as the big man pointed. The fact that he hadn't been tied was evidence that the marshal was confident of his ability with the revolver should Morgan have ideas of escaping.

They got down in front of a red brick building that had elegant curved window tops and heavy shutters painted gray-green. The building looked strong enough to withstand cannon fire.

There were offices inside, a long hallway that led to the back and stairs to the second floor. The large office on the right as they entered had a frosted glass door and the legend in gold leaf: United States Marshal James Elkland.

Morgan said, "Is that you, Marshal Elkland?"

"That's me." Elkland opened the door and ushered him inside. "Have a chair." He went around the desk and sat down as Morgan examined the room. It had a dozen framed pictures on the walls, a rack of rifles, a huge elk head and antlers and a sideboard that had undoubtedly come across the plains from the east. Elkland got down some forms and studied them, finally selecting one.

He said, "I'm told you hold a commission in the United States Army . . . is that true?"

"Yes. Colonel."

"Colonel! Well. That's very interesting in view of the fact that you were a Confederate officer. There's a law, you know."

Morgan shrugged. "General Pomfret can do amazing things. It was a surprise to me too."

"I can imagine. Was that Pomfret you were with in the restaurant?"

"Yes, it was."

Marshal Elkland took a pen and wrote on the form. He glanced up at Morgan. "Sorry 'bout this, but I'm going to have to put you in a cell for the night."

"I understand."

"In the morning we'll send you back to Kansas City."

"What's the charge against me?"

"At the moment it's murder. But I doubt if it will stand." Elkland gave him what Morgan suspicioned was a rare smile. "Of course the judge is annoyed with you — or so I hear. He's a stickler for fact and form."

"But I *was* attacked and only defended myself."

"Yes, I know. As I told you, I read the report. Between us, if it were me you wouldn't be under arrest. Unfortunately, I'm not the judge and I'm under his orders. I do what I'm told." He rose. "Let's go along to the jail."

It was a reasonably clean cell but cold and dusty as a box of potatoes. It had a stone floor, gray and uninviting, a heavy beamed ceiling, an iron cot with a wisp of mattress and a blanket folded at one end, no chair and a tiny opening that was possibly called a window. The opening gave no light and was much too high for him to see out.

He flopped on the cot and drew the blanket over him and drifted off to sleep.

In the morning he discovered there were five other prisoners on the row, coughing and hacking and muttering to themselves, bitching because they had no tobacco.

The turnkey came and pulled three from the cells. Morgan thought they looked like the town drunks.

The fourth man's cell was at the far end. He set up a clamor and when the turnkey shouted at him to shut up, he yelled back that the man in the next cell was dead.

That proved to be true.

The undertaker was sent for and several men rolled the corpse onto a stretcher and carried it out with considerable swearing. The deceased had no money at all and the undertaker complained that the county never paid him enough to bury anyone properly.

The prisoner at the end then began to sing doleful songs in a whiskey voice, mostly about a woman who didn't love him anymore.

Morgan thought she showed good sense.

He was taken from the cell in the middle of the morning, given a plate of beans, some bread and a cup of tepid coffee, then hustled to Marshal Elkland's office.

Elkland and two men were waiting for him. The man put heavy manacles on his wrists behind his back and the marshal said, "You'll go by the next train. Good luck." He nodded to the men.

Frank Willis rode into Kingston early in the afternoon and quickly learned about the shooting of a man named Corry Baker. According to the newspaper account, Baker had accosted a "John Smith" in a local saloon and been knocked about. Baker had later come after Smith with a gun at the railroad station and had been shot down.

Was the man with the unlikely handle of "John Smith" really Shelter Morgan? The deputy sheriff's description of him seemed to indicate it. Smith was obviously a very slick gunman. He had taken care of Baker in a very professional way. Just like Morgan had shot Keno Willis.

And then John Smith had boarded the train and presumably had gone on to Kansas City.

Frank Willis left his horse at the local livery stable and bought a ticket. He would be back, he told the livery man. He took the train with some misgivings because Kansas City was a big town. He might easily lose the trail there.

When he reached Kansas City—the largest town he had ever seen—his hopes plummeted. Where the hell would he even start to look?

A block or two from the station he found a row of boarding houses and took a room, debating whether or not to give up the chase. He must easily be a week behind Morgan. Hell, the man could be halfway to San Francisco—or he could have returned to Toland.

He ate a greasy meal in a nearby restaurant and went to the room to lie on the bed, staring at the ceiling. Yes, might as well swallow his anger and give it all up. Poor Keno would never be avenged. There was no goddamned justice in the world, not for poor folks.

In the morning he dragged himself out of bed and pulled on his boots. He went back to the restaurant and sat at the counter. Someone had left a newspaper and as he turned the pages his eye was caught by a name:

SHELTER MORGAN accused of murder! Ex-Confederate officer indicted in shooting of four men on Kansas City street. Morgan pleads self defense.

There was much more and Willis read it with rising excitement. He hadn't lost the trail after all!

73

CHAPTER NINE

There was a hearing and two witnesses came forth to testify that Morgan had drawn his weapon and fired on the four horsemen and that *they* were the victims.

Morgan stared at them, two poorly dressed men who professed to being bricklayers and had seen the action as they went home for the day. Morgan's lawyer asked them why they had come forward and they replied they were public-spirited. The lawyer inferred they were being paid to testify and they reacted with anger.

But in a private meeting, the lawyer said, "It will go poorly for us in front of a jury if they continue with those lies." He was a young man, slim and pale with sunken cheeks and sparse black hair. It was probably impossible at this date to round up any credible witness who saw the gunfight. The two assailants who were in custody would naturally agree with the bricklayers, though their testimony might not be believed by a reasonably smart jury.

"When it comes to trial," the lawyer said, "I may be able to shake them up. You say they were *not* there. They may get tangled up with the details. Anything we can do to make the jury suspect they are frauds is in our favor."

"How long will it take to come to trial?"

The lawyer shrugged. "Hard to say. Maybe six months."

Morgan leaned back and closed his eyes. Six months in jail! It was an eternity. And no guarantee that he would be free of the law even then. The law had hooks and claws and once they set into a man, they seemingly hated to give him up . . . innocent or not.

He was taken back to a cell and sat in semi-darkness for a long time, wondering if Pomfret would move heaven and earth to get him out. But even Pomfret had limits. The hearing lasted two days.

After the hearing he was put into the jail cell for another night, then transferred to another jail facility just outside the city. It was an older group of buildings, painted a dull brown, with a stockade fence of sharpened palings and guards walking the perimeter, looking down into the yard.

The second day he was there, General Pomfret showed up. They faced each other across a wide table with a guard sitting by the door of the room. Pomfret said, "If it were anything but a murder charge we'd have you out. I've been talking to your attorney and he is investigating the two witnesses. If he can prove they are being paid, you'll be out in a hurry."

"Of course they're being paid."

"I'll try to get your trial date moved up."

"Thanks. How was the parade?"

"In Topeka? It went off without a hitch. But he's already moved on and now he's talking about a hunting party." Pomfret shook his head. "He says he was a hunter in his youth. He wants to get out on a horse and shoot a deer or something. The reporters will love it . . ."

The door guard stood up and jingled his keys. Pomfret glanced at him. "Well, time's up. What can I send you?"

"How about Amanda Bates."

"Yes, I don't wonder."

The criminal population was low in the facility, called the Rathole by the inmates, but named the Ralph Peterson County Jail. Morgan was given a small cell to himself.

His first day in the general exercise yard he was tested by a man named Big Mike Pukanski. Pukanski faced him, with a crowd of eager faces in a half circle, watching. "We gettin' meat t'night in the messhall. You gi'me yours."

Morgan looked him over, big muscles, a shiny, flat face, cauliflower ears, doubtless the jail bully. He smiled. "What kind of meat?"

"Who cares whut kind?" Big Mike's finger jabbed Morgan's chest. "You gimme yours."

Morgan grabbed the finger, bent it back and there was a loud crack as the bone snapped. Mike screamed and jumped, stamping up and down, holding the hurt hand. Three of his cronies shouted for a guard, yelling Big Mike needed the doctor.

Morgan noticed grins on a dozen faces as they watched the big man being taken out of the yard. One of them said, "I been hopin' t'see somethin' like that fer a year."

But another sidled up, "You made some enemies, friend. From now on, watch yore back."

"I've watched it all my life," Morgan said.

Big Mike was in the infirmary for several hours and when he returned to his cell he was pale, with a heavy bandage on his hand. That evening, in the messhall, he sat at the same rough-hewn table with Morgan and said nothing about the meat Morgan was eating. But if glowers could kill, Morgan would have been dog food.

In his cell that evening, Morgan made up his mind. The judicial system had made an error and, since it ground so slowly, it would take months of his life to get itself sorted out. It cared nothing for him.

So—he would escape, and worry about right and wrong another time. He began to look about him with different eyes.

There were several men who had been in the jail for years and he struck up a conversation with one, a man named Shelby. He was skinny and bent, with shifty eyes that never looked at the man he talked to. He had been in dozens of prisons and jails, he told Morgan; he was a burglar by trade, what some called a second-story man. He climbed the outsides of buildings and went in windows when people were asleep.

"How can I get out of this place?" Morgan asked him.

"Go over the wall."

"Can it be done?"

Shelby's eyes shifted back and forth as he hesitated. They were in the exercise yard, hands deep in pockets, backs to one side of the wall. "Probably at night—maybe at night."

"Is there no other way?"

"There's other ways . . . but we got no guns and no horses when we get out."

"Has anyone made it out?"

Shelby hunched his shoulders. "A few."

"How did they do it?"

"They got away when they was working outside. They had help from friends. You got to have help."

Morgan nodded, thinking about Pomfret. Would the general help him break out of jail? It might go against all Pomfret's training.

There were work gangs that were taken outside under guard every day. They worked in a large vegetable garden or in the fields surrounding the jail, which was self supporting in the matter of food, except for meat. Everyone wanted to get on one of the gangs to relieve the monotony, if for no other reason. It was several days before Morgan's name was called.

He was led outside the walls with ten or twelve others and three mounted deputies armed with pistols and rifles pointed to a road and they marched along it. When they came to a cornfield there was a shed with tools and each man took a long handled hoe and they were put to chopping weeds.

Morgan found it easy work; the guards lolled on the horses, watching them casually, smoking cigars, now and then exchanging banter with one or two of the prisoners.

Morgan examined his surroundings. The cornfield stretched away for nearly half a mile, or so it seemed, reaching toward a horizon of low blue hills. There were no towns nearby, the Kansas River was somewhere to the north. With a fast horse, he thought, he might evade pursuit, enough to lose himself in the brakes. After that he could work his way west and with a bit of luck, join Pomfret.

When the shadows began to lengthen, the guards ordered all the tools returned to the shed; they were carefully counted to make sure no one had hidden one. Then they were formed up and marched back to the jail compound.

The jail food, less than he had ever eaten except in his previous prison sentence, tasted good that night after the hours of steady work. His muscles ached a bit but he knew in several days he would be even more fit. Hard work never killed anyone—where had he heard that?

As he walked back to his cell from the messhall he was suddenly attacked by two friends of Big Mike. He knew their nicknames, Soddy and Mack. Soddy was a man as big as himself, with sloping shoulders and an ugly, flat face. Mack was slimmer and it was rumored that he was a knife man. They jostled him up against the wall and he saw half a dozen men hurry to group themselves so the guard could not see. Any fight was entertainment.

Morgan caught a glimpse of a knifeblade and he

kicked out instantly, catching Mack in the groin. The knife went flying to clatter on the stone floor beyond the fringe of men. He heard a guard yell as he grasped Soddy's arm, took several steps and flung the man with all his strength. Soddy slammed into the brick wall with his back and his head hit with a terrible sound, as if a melon had been split. He was dead, Morgan knew, before the body hit the floor. Mack lay doubled up in a fetal position, moaning.

"Get back! Git in the goddam cells!" Three guards came running, shoving the cons away. One pushed Morgan's back to the wall. "You stand there."

One guard bent over Soddy for a moment then shook his head. "He's dead as hell."

"You saw it all," Morgan said.

"I seen the knife," the guard said. "That fuckin' Mack'll cut—" He motioned Morgan, "into yore cell, right now."

A dozen prisoners had seen the confrontation and several yelled that Soddy had got what was coming to him. Another yelled to the guards to let him out and he'd kick Mack in the balls too. Others laughed.

Mack was carried into his cell and lay there without moving.

The body was rolled onto a stretcher and lugged out and the cellblock was abuzz with conversation long after lights out. Men shouted to Morgan, saying he'd done what everyone wanted to do; they hated Soddy and were glad he was dead.

In the middle of the next morning a guard came for Morgan and he was taken to a small square room and seated on a bench and told to wait. In about a half hour the superintendent, Harry Wilkes, and two men in guard uniforms filed in and sat opposite. One had a large pad of paper and some sharpened pencils. The other was one of the corridor guards.

Wilkes said, "Write this down, with the time and date. We are questioning the prisoner, Shelter Morgan, and the guard, Bert Hamm. This concerns the fight between Morgan and the man known as Soddy—we'll fill in his real name later, and the man, Mack Brown. Same with his name. Let the record show that Soddy died in the fight."

He looked at Morgan. "Now, you relate the fight as you saw it. Tell us ever'thing that happened."

Morgan nodded. "The fight is because I broke Big Mike's finger earlier."

"That's Big Mike Pukanski?"

"Yes sir. He crowded me and I had to stop him."

"Go on."

"I was coming back from the messhall when Soddy and Mack shoved me up against the wall and I saw Mack's knife. So I fought back."

The superintendent stared at him for a moment. "You disabled one man and killed another. Is that what you mean by 'you fought back'?"

"I knew Mack's reputation, sir. And I was sure that Soddy was set to break something . . ." Morgan shrugged. "Simple retaliation."

"All right." Wilkes turned to the guard. "What did you see, Hamm."

"Well sir, I heard a shout, and when I stood up I could see Soddy and Mack going after Morgan. The men was crowding around, but I seen the knife all right. Then it come flying out and Mack

81

doubled up. Then I seen Soddy slammed up against the wall."

Wilkes glanced at the man writing busily. "All right. Who attacked who?"

Hamm said quickly, "Oh, Soddy and Mack attacked Morgan, sir. I seen that clear enough."

"So you would say it was self defense?"

"Yes sir. Two men on one."

The superintendent nodded. "Is there anything else you want to add, Morgan?"

Morgan smiled. "Yes sir. I'd like to get out of here."

Wilkes twitched his facial muscles in what might have been a smile. "I expect you would." He motioned to the scribe. "When you finish that, have them sign it and bring it to me."

"Yes sir."

The next day the body of Soddy was buried without ceremony in the jail plot. No one wept.

Two days later, in the cornfield, Morgan saw his chance. He had been edging closer to the perimeter of the field, apparently concentrating on the job, and one of the guards, a tall mustached man with red hair and sallow horseface, drifted closer, the rifle across his thighs. He was several hundred feet from the other guards mounted on a roan horse.

Out of the corner of his eye, Morgan saw the man turn his head to spit tobacco juice, and in that instant, Morgan struck.

With the hoe handle, he jabbed the man's neck and swept him off the horse. Quickly he grabbed the holstered revolver and brought it down along the side of the guard's head.

He swung into the saddle and dug in his heels. He was a hundred yards away, galloping the animal through the rows of corn stalks before another guard noticed.

Shouting in surprise, the guard emptied his rifle at the fleeing man and spurred his horse.

Morgan never looked back until he was a mile away, heading into the low, brushy hills. He was elated! He suddenly had a horse and a pistol. But no more ammunition than was in the gun. However, there was a cloth-covered tin canteen slung alongside the pommel and a cloth sack of food tied behind the cantle. Things were looking up.

The pursuit gave up before the guard reached the hills, possibly realizing, Morgan thought, that one man wasn't enough for the job. He'd go back and wire ahead. From a hill, Morgan watched him turn back. He'd catch hell from the superintendent.

Morgan headed west, steering by the sun. The horse was a good animal, not the best, but sturdy; and the saddle was an old army McClellan in reasonable condition. He was wearing a gray prison uniform, the shirt had: County Jail stenciled on the back. It would be an excellent idea to get rid of it as soon as he could.

He rode steadily throughout the day seeing no one, or no sign of habitation. The land was undulating prairie crossed by sandy washes. When it began to grow dark he got down in a canebrake and ate the food in the sack without a fire. Cold beef and bread and an apple.

There was sure to be a pursuit. They would certainly alert all county sheriffs by telegraph; there might even be a reward offered. He *was* charged with murder, after all.

He slept for several hours, then got up and traveled on.

The next day he had to make a wide detour to avoid a small crossroads town. Sitting the horse a mile or more from the distant buildings, he debated whether or not to wait for darkness, then enter the town to obtain other clothes . . . and food.

But he decided not to waste the hours. He went on. It was important to get as much distance between him and the law as possible. When night fell he was tired to death and halted in a sandy draw to sleep while the roan horse cropped grass. He woke long before dawn, stretched and went on doggedly. He was hungry, he needed a shave and he was tired of running. What would he give for a bath!

He smiled when he saw lights in the distance. They were few, glimmering on the horizon like beacons of hope. They turned out to be five buildings clustered on a flat plain by a sluggish stream, in the middle of nowhere.

He picketed the horse by the stream and went ahead on foot, the revolver tucked in his belt. One of the buildings was a deadfall, a tent-shaped room built of unplaned boards with a sign printed in grease on the front: Saloon. Inside someone was singing raucously to a guitar accompaniment . . . a song about a girl who didn't love him.

Another building was a general store, one a harness shop with a blacksmith's shed attached, one a dry goods store and the last apparently a boarding house. All were dark and closed but the saloon.

Morgan silently circled the dry goods store, wanting to put an elbow through the glass window. He desperately needed other clothes.

He decided against the idea finally; there was a very good possibility that the owner lived in the back of the store and might easily meet him with a shotgun as he came through. He found a dark patch of shadow near the saloon instead and settled down to wait.

It was nearly an hour before a man came out, navigating unsteadily, heading for the boarding house. He was about the right size, Morgan thought, wearing a dark coat and a bowler hat.

Following him, Morgan pressed the revolver muzzle into his back and steered him out into the prairie, silencing the man's protests. "Do as you're told and shut up."

"What the hell you want? I ain't got no money!"

A good distance away, Morgan halted him. "Take off the coat and shirt."

"What?"

"You heard me. Take 'em off." He lifted the bowler and put it on his own head. He had never worn one.

"Whut the hell . . ."

"I told you to shut up!" Morgan clicked back the hammer and looked ugly.

The man shucked the coat in a hurry. "You the goddamndest robber I ever seen."

"Take off the shirt."

Grumbling, the victim pulled it off over his head.

Morgan grabbed it, "Now git!" The man stumbled away as Morgan hurried to the roan horse and loped into the dark, leaving the half naked man to stare after him in bafflement.

In a mile or so he halted, pulled off the prison shirt and tossed it away. The victim's shirt fit passably well. The coat was a bit too tight but it was warm; better than nothing.

God! The things he did for Pomfret!

CHAPTER TEN

A short distance outside the town of Slidell there was a pass, a deep cut made by the engineers when the track was laid, through which the presidential train must go. Gavin Bowers thought it a perfect spot for an ambush. It was far enough away from the town so that an explosion would not be heard, in the middle of the formless prairie, but with a river not far off. The river was part of his plan.

"Fred will blow up the engine in the pass," he said to Jordan. "It'll take all the powder we have but we'll be on the hill and will have a good shot at hitting the President."

"What d'you mean all the powder we have?"

"He could only find ten sticks."

"There was plenty in Topeka."

"Jesus! Stop with the horseshit! Who wants to carry dynamite on a horse for two hundred fucking miles!"

"It could be old stuff," Fred said. "Too goddamn unstable."

Jordan subsided. He was a lanky man with bristling brows and a mean mouth. He had spent nine years of his life in a territorial prison and it had colored his view of most everything. He said, "Then we take the boat across the river?"

"That's right. Then we smash the boats. We'll have horses waiting. There isn't a ford for fifty miles and it's too fast and dirty to swim."

Fred asked, "How much time we got?"

"Maybe four days." Bowers pointed at him. "You take care of the dynamite. Jordan and I will arrange the horses and come back in the boat."

"All right," Fred said. He was an old timer, skinny and weathered. He had learned explosives in the war and had lost only three fingers of his left hand. Fuses could be tricky.

A posse caught up with Morgan in a series of low sand hills. Doubtless, as he had feared, the jail officials had wired ahead and this group had come out from a nearby town and happened to ride in the right direction. But their luck ran out at that point. They started firing at him too soon.

Morgan turned the roan horse and galloped away between two rounded hills with bullets cracking around him. They had come upon him an hour before dusk and he was able to evade them until full dark.

They ran him out of the hills into the rolling prairie and could not track him after sundown. The deputy sheriff in charge decided to make camp while they still had his trail, and go again in the morning.

They ought to be able to run one man down, he told them.

Morgan circled around and came up on them as they settled down with a fire. Picketing the roan in a draw, he crept up on the camp, close enough to listen to their chatter. They were elated they'd run onto him and talked about what they'd do with the reward money, five hundred dollars.

Morgan made a face. Five hundred! Well, not bad.

The smell of food, as they cooked it, was distracting. His stomach had long been protesting the lack. But in an hour they let the fire die and, posting a lookout, curled up in blankets and went to sleep.

Morgan was patient. He waited till the guard changed. Most would be well asleep then and would wake blearily after two hours sleep. The new guard walked around the camp, a rifle over his shoulder, listening to the far-off bark of foxes. It was no trick at all for Morgan to creep up behind him and lay the revolver barrel across his skull, enough to make him sleep. He caught the man as he fell, then took the money from his pockets, the rifle and cartridge belt, a hat and a food sack he found by the fire. He left the bowler.

Then he cut the picket ropes to set the horses free. Mounting the roan, he yelled and slapped the hat and drove the horses onto the dark prairie in a stampede. It would take them hours to round up one or two. They would not spend the reward money *that* easily.

* * *

In another day and a half he came to the little town of Wister. To call it a town was to be generous. It had no telegraph and got newspapers once a week from the next town, Kalber, farther north. Kalber printed a weekly, gleaning national news from Topeka papers, most of which was uninteresting to them.

The railroad, Morgan was told by a storekeeper, was about fifty miles to the north and the nearest station was Fairview.

"If you's going there, you kin cut across the prairie till you hit the tracks. Then turn right'r left."

"Right or left?"

"Well, it depends on which way you is from the town. If'n you turn right and it's left, then you'll go a fer piece."

"You mean it's a guessing game."

"Um. Unless you takes the road."

"Well," Morgan said with relief. "I'll take the road."

"Umm. The road goes to Deever. It ain't a station. The train don't stop there 'less it's an emergency."

"Well, which way is Fairview from Deever?"

"Oh, to the left. You got to go left from Deever." The storekeeper pointed. "It maybe ten mile. Could be eleven or twelve. I don't think anybody ever measured it." He looked over his glasses to Morgan. "They had a measurin' wheel out here one day, come from Kalber. Kalber's just sixty two mile thataway." He jerked his thumb. "Exactly. Well, by the road."

"I see."

The storekeeper smiled. "But you go over the prairie you can't miss the tracks. You sure you ain't lost?"

"No," Morgan said, "I'm here. How could I be lost?"

The storekeeper had a week-old newspaper but it was very little help. It had items about the President's visit but it did not outline his itinerary. Morgan had no idea if the train had already passed Fairview or was yet to see it.

He bought food, put it in a sack and left the town behind.

He went directly across the prairie, not taking the road, following the storekeeper's directions. It was a long way to the tracks and when he came to them he turned left. In three days he was in Fairview and the President's train had not arrived.

It was a small burg and had no hotel. He put up in a stall of the livery stable, bought a bath and shave and began to feel himself again.

Pomfret would be astonished to see him. And perhaps so would a few others. The newspaper he bought in Fairview said that he was a wanted man. $500.00 reward for information leading to the arrest and incarceration of Shelter Morgan. There was no picture of him. Someone had made a drawing that showed a devilish looking man staring out at the world, but it looked nothing like him.

As he came from the local cafe after breakfast the next morning he noticed the crowd gathering in front of the telegraph office. The telegrapher had just put up a notice. The President's train had been dynamited outside of Slidell. The tracks were destroyed and until they could be replaced the train would not be coming.

Morgan inquired. "How far is Slidell?"

The stationmaster said it was 90 miles, by the tracks.

Morgan set out in an hour, following the tracks. The stationmaster had shown him a map which showed the tracks making a large curve following high ground. He could probably cut a day's travel time by cutting across at the little town of Tema and picking up the tracks again near Slidell.

It took him a day and a half to reach Tema, which was only a water stop; there was no town, only a cluster of shacks and one railroad building housing the man who kept the water tower in condition.

He pushed into the prairie that afternoon and made camp at night in the shelter of a rock jumble—where others had camped before him. The next day he reached Slidell.

It was a tiny burg, bleached by the sun, its only reason for being to serve the railroad. It had a roundhouse and other railroad buildings and not much else except a six room hotel and a cafe, and three saloons.

He found Pomfret in one of the rooms, writing letters. When he knocked on the door and the general opened it, he did not at first recognize him. Morgan said, "It's me, General. Can I come in?"

"Jesus Christ!" Pomfret said, one of the few times Morgan had ever heard him swear. "Where did you drop from?"

Morgan closed the door behind him. "I escaped. What did you expect?"

Pomfret sat down heavily. "You escaped?"

"Haven't you read the papers? It's in all of them."

Pomfret shook his head. "I didn't think you'd escape!"

"I'm worth five hundred dollars. Tell me what I've missed. I hear the railroad track's been blown up."

"Yes, someone tried to blow up the train—we think. But they cut the fuse too short and it blew up the tracks before the engine arrived. Then shots were fired at the President's car, but it was protected and no real harm was done. How did you escape?"

"I made off with a horse while I was on a work gang. So how is the President?"

"He's hunting."

"What?"

"He insisted on going hunting. He's been gone three days with a large party, including some troops."

Morgan shook his head. "That's the way to go hunting, with cavalry."

Pomfret got up and poured whiskey into two glasses, handing Morgan one. "What are we going to do with you?"

"What d'you mean?"

"As soon as someone recognizes you they'll turn you in for the reward, won't they? Five hundred is a lot of money to a lot of people."

"Is it to you?"

"Well, I won't turn you in, if that's what you mean."

"Who did the dynamiting?"

"Probably Gavin Bowers. Who else?"

"What have you done about it?"

"*I* haven't done anything about it. I told you long ago, I'm not responsible for guarding the President. He's got the military for that. But men were thicker than flies at a picnic, all over the ground and they found evidence of several who had fired on the cars, but not much else. Luckily the President wasn't hurt."

"And they got away . . ."

"Yes. Across the river. Probably they had a boat stashed and rowed across."

"Not so good. And of course there's no proof that it was Bowers."

"No. None. But who else?"

Morgan shrugged. "Persistent, isn't he?"

"Very." Pomfret sipped the liquor and frowned at the glass. "You've got to stay undercover, Shel. There are people here who will recognize you—Congressman Bates for one."

"He's here?"

"Yes. In this very hotel."

"Is Amanda with him?"

"Certainly."

Morgan drank and paced the room. He put the glass down. "What kind of law in this town?"

"A town marshal. He looks competent. He has no authority outside the town, of course. But if he could, he would jail you and wire the county sheriff. I'm sure you're a walking fortune to him."

Morgan growled.

Pomfret said, "If he suspects you're here he'll get a posse together."

Morgan continued to pace. Being on the run from the law certainly made things harder. And the gen-

94

eral was right. There were any number of people in the President's party who would recognize him at sight, and many who might need five hundred dollars. Probably this very hotel was full of them. How many had gone on the hunting trip?

Halting, he frowned at Pomfret. "In your opinion, is the President safe where he is? Is there any way Bowers could get at him?"

"I doubt it. He's surrounded by trusted men and Bowers has no idea where they are. No one knows their itinerary because I'm certain they don't know it themselves. They'll go where they think they can find game."

"So you say it's possible that Gavin Bowers doesn't even know the President *is* on a hunting trip."

"Yes, certainly. There's been no public announcement. I'm sure most think he's waiting in the hotel for the tracks to be repaired."

Nodding, Morgan sat down and picked up the glass. Then he could devote his time to worrying about his own ass.

Amanda wouldn't tell on him, would she?

Morgan stayed in Pomfret's rooms the rest of the day. The general had food sent up, saying he had no time to go to a restaurant. But after dark Morgan buckled on the Colt and, feeling shut in and restless, stepped into the hall intending to go down the back steps to his horse in the stable.

As he reached the end of the hall where the stairs were, a door opened and a surprised voice said,

"Shel!"

He turned, looking into the astonished face of Amanda. Her arms went out to him as she smiled. "Come in . . . come in!"

CHAPTER ELEVEN

Glancing along the deserted hallway, Morgan stepped into the room. It was very small, a bed and chair and chest of drawers. She grasped his arms. "Where have you been? The papers say you were sent to jail." She bolted the door behind him.

"It was all a mistake."

"People have been saying awful things about you—that you're a gunfighter, and worse."

"I'm a very bad character," Morgan said seriously. "Where's your father?"

"In the next room—only he's not there now. Did you escape from jail?"

He nodded. "Can you keep it a secret?"

Her hands moved up and down on his arms, squeezing slightly. "Oh yes . . ." She moved close, her arms sliding around him, her pelvis pushing . . . a little harder . . . He bent his head and kissed her, discovering all at once that she was no innocent. Why did he think of Pomfret all of a sudden? Her kisses were insistent and she moaned a bit, pulling at him, tugging at his clothes.

He scooped her up and laid her on the bed, crawling up beside her. He unbuckled the gunbelt and let it slide to the floor, thump. With both hands she tore at his buttons and got his jeans open, then slid inside to grasp him. He slid her skirt and petticoats up, kissing her the while, caressing her white thighs and she gasped and sucked in her breath as his hand moved upward. She pulled at him. . . . "Please—please—please—"

He moved between her knees and held her in a fierce embrace, feeling her legs come up on either side of him as he entered her. She said, "Ahhhhhh . . ." and began to writhe as he stroked into her. The bed squeaked and protested . . .

Then she jerked and nearly cried out and for several moments he threshed . . . then the raging sea receded, and he gradually became still, resting in her arms, his lips pressed to her cheek.

They remained still for a long while, her legs tight about him. Then suddenly someone rapped on the door. She started, then her finger found his lips and pressed. The rapping continued for half a minute, then footsteps went away.

She whispered. "It's father." She gave a long sigh. "Now I must dress and hurry downstairs and pretend I was there . . ."

He rolled off her and she said, "Where are you staying?"

"I don't know."

"You can spend the night here—if you go early enough."

He smiled at her. "Don't think I won't consider it."

"Then if you come, knock twice, then twice again so I'll know it's you."

He got off the bed and put himself together, buckling on the pistol. She smoothed her skirts and went to the mirror as he unbolted the door. She ran to him, kissing him hotly. "Please, I'll see you again . . . ?"

He smiled. "I'll be back." He patted her rump and slipped from the room.

He went down the back stairs quickly; the hotel seemed deserted, not a sound except for someone snoring as he passed a door. He opened the back door and breathed deeply the cold air and for a moment he leaned against the door, eyes closed. What a wild and passionate little thing she was! Was she one of those women he had heard about—who couldn't help their unnatural desires? Would she be the same with any man? He smiled ruefully to himself. Probably. He wondered if her father knew, had any idea what his daughter was. Maybe—maybe not.

There was a lantern hanging high on a nail, glowing softly just inside the stable. He lifted it down and went along the stalls looking for the roan horse.

Satisfied that the stableboy was caring for the animal, he put the lantern back and walked out to the quiet street, pausing in the deep shadows. Several saloons were still lighted and music flowed from them. Where was Gavin Bowers? If he hoped to harm the President, he should be nearby.

Maybe he was in a strategy meeting this very moment with Congressman Bates.

He roamed the town, prowling through the saloons, but saw no sign of Bowers. He knew there was little chance of finding him but he had to do it. Finally he went back to the hotel and rapped lightly on Amanda's door as she had told him. She opened it and pulled him in.

He rather enjoyed the feeling of bedding the congressman's daughter. She was enormously demanding, saying she wanted payment for the bed. He was glad to settle the bill. She was obviously very experienced at the game; how astonished Pomfret would be.

At dawn he slid out of bed and dressed quietly, letting himself out of the room before she woke. A small restaurant across from the hotel was open and he had bacon and eggs there, dawdling over coffee. If Bowers was in the town he must be holed up in a house somewhere and if so, he could stay there indefinitely and no one would find him.

But he might be camped outside the town somewhere. Why not take a look? He went back across the street and around to the stable. He was saddling the roan horse when a man stepped into the stable with a drawn revolver.

"You're Shelter Morgan."

Morgan turned slowly, eyeing the gun. "My name is John Blake. You've made a mistake, friend."

The other smiled thinly. "No, I've seen you several times with General Pomfret. You're Morgan all right. And you're five hundred dollars to me." He motioned with the pistol. "Leave the horse be. We'll just go along to the marshal's office." He backed slowly. "Come out here and turn around."

Morgan stepped into the yard and the man took his gun.

"All right, now walk ahead of me."

Morgan was forced to do as he said. He went around the hotel and down the boardwalk to the small stone building that housed the town marshal's office and jail.

But when they got there, the office was locked. The man swore. "Damnit, he must be out somewhere."

He glanced along the empty street and Morgan's backhand caught him alongside the cheekbone. It snapped the man's head back and Morgan grabbed the pistol from nerveless fingers. He dragged the limp figure around to the side of the building and used the man's belt to tie his hands. He shoved one gun into the holster and the other into his belt and hurried along the walk again to the stable. Damn! Now the man would spread the news that he was here in town.

He smoothed the blanket on the roan's back, threw on the saddle and cinched it up. Lady Luck was dealing from the bottom of the pack today. What the hell had he ever done to her?

Mounting, he rode into the prairie.

It was a dark night when Gavin Bowers rowed back across the river with lanky Jordan and old

Fred. They hid the boat as best they could in some brush and hiked into the town, a weary journey. Fred knew of a deserted shack on the outskirts and they went there, glad to get out of the chill.

Bowers felt down in the mouth. They had failed miserably in trying to blow up the train. The goddamned blasting powder had gone off prematurely—old Fred said it was a defective fuse. He had also been surprised at how well the President was guarded. And with what energy. A bunch of soldiers had pursued them hotly, firing at them all the way to the river. They had barely gotten away.

He liked the idea of dynamiting the train but it was a difficult problem. How to cut the fuse? It depended on how fast the train was going . . . and that was guesswork, of course. Old Fred thought it nearly impossible to guess the speed of the train and the speed of the fuse so they would both come together at the same time, and explode. It was no problem to blow up the track, but all that did was delay the train. Old Fred said if there was a good curve somewhere they could surely derail the train and pile it up in the ditch. But this was flat prairie and no curves that would do.

So he would have to come up with a new plan. He was very annoyed to learn, when Jordan came back from buying food supplies in town, that the President was off on a hunting trip. According to the talk, the President had gone hunting while the track was being repaired. Bowers swore. They had missed a good chance!

And now to find the hunting party on the vast prairie was probably impossible; they might be anywhere.

All in all it was no easy task to eliminate such a man. He had had no idea of the complexity of the problem — nor probably had his father.

The problem was getting worse. The newspapers across the land had carried the story of the dynamiting as a threat to the chief executive's life. It was only a few years since Abraham Lincoln had been shot. Of course some papers regarded the bombing as only a warning, but Bowers knew the security net had been tightened.

But the worst blow to him was still to come. Jordan returned from the general store in town the next day with food supplies and a poster he'd torn from a telegraph pole. Copies of the poster were being put up everywhere, he said. Bowers swore a blue streak on seeing it. There were two pictures of him on the sheet, one with a beard and one without.

Across the top of the paper were the words: WANTED $1000.00 REWARD!

General Pomfret had sent to St. Louis for the posters, urging haste in their manufacture. This was done while Morgan was in jail in Kansas City.

The delivery of the first boxes of posters came soon after Morgan showed up in Slidell. Pomfret paid several boys to tack them up in front of every saloon and on telegraph poles in and out of town.

Morgan returned to town after dark and, on seeing them said to Pomfret, "Are you afraid you'll drive him farther underground?"

"Yes, but I care less about catching him than I do

about the President's safety."

"If you do catch him, what'll you charge him with?"

Pomfret grunted. "I'll think of something."

The President's hunting party returned to the town only a day before the tracks were repaired and ready for use. Excellent timing, which showed which side Lady Luck was on. Instead of going to the hotel, the President took up residence in his private car, and the next day the train moved out.

The next stop was Fairview.

Morgan went across country, retracing his steps, and arrived the day after the train, which was put onto a siding.

Preparations for a county fair was in the making when Morgan had been in the town before, but he'd paid no attention since he was leaving immediately. Now the fair was in full bloom and the President's arrival only increased the excitement. The fairgrounds were just outside the town, a great sprawling area with tents and hastily-erected buildings for sideshows and games, and a large oval racetrack.

People thronged into the town from outlying districts, as much to catch a glimpse of the President as to attend the fair. It was prominently announced that the President would personally present the grand winners in the public contests with their prizes.

It was a grand headache for the security people.

Morgan had started a mustache the day he stole the horse and got away from the county jail. Now it was thick enough to change his face so that a casual observer would pass over him. The daguerreotype that had been printed was not large and it had been forgotten by most, surely. So he walked the fairgrounds without worrying.

Pomfret had the Bowers WANTED posters tacked up here and there about the grounds, and had been able to use his influence to prevent posters of Morgan being tacked up as well. Morgan did not inquire too deeply about those things. Pomfret had his methods.

A kind of stage had been built with benches for spectators, and from this platform the President would hand out the prizes. It would not be an easy place to guard — and had not been built with that in mind. None of the locals had any idea an assassination might be attempted.

Morgan walked the platform examining the places where a rifleman might lie in wait. There were a number. The man in charge of guarding the President was Colonel Ernest Hobby, a youngish man, West Pointer, whose father had been a hero of the war. Some said the colonel had his job by influence, but he was an intense and clever man and thus far he had made no mistakes.

Morgan talked to him about the platform and Hobby agreed that his men would occupy each of the suspicious positions themselves during the time the President was in danger. Hobby also agreed to station men at every fairground entrance and exit to watch for Bowers. Everything that could be done, was being done.

Maybe Bowers had decided to give up the idea. But Pomfret thought not. "Bowers and his father are fanatics. Do not underestimate them."

The first great event was a series of horse races which filled the spectator areas with milling, shouting people. Eight races were held and afterward a wagon race was announced. Each wagon was pulled by a two horse team. It proved to be a rough, smashing contest in which two wagons were nearly destroyed — but the crowd loved the excitement of it.

Morgan wandered the grounds, poking into everything without result. There were bars and in several were girls performing the oldest trade; there were dancers in as scanty dress as allowable; there were various sideshows and exhibits — but no Bowers. He had to be somewhere . . .

He was somewhere, riding from Slidell across the vast prairie with Jordan and Fred. They missed the town and finally came back to find it when they came to the railroad tracks and realized they must be far beyond. The prairie was like a sea; it was impossible to see more than a few miles in any direction and one easily became lost.

His luck was running poorly, Bowers thought, swearing at the extra miles. But he had no idea how poorly until he met the troopers. They were close to the town when a cavalry patrol surprised them, and when they attempted to run, fired a volley over their heads. A young lieutenant wanted to know why they had bolted, and was unsatisfied with Bowers' explanation. The lieutenant thought Bowers looked familiar and took the three of them in to the deputy sheriff who recognized Bowers at once. Bowers was quickly placed in a jail cell.

However, the two men with him were released. Neither was a fugitive, apparently. The taller man swore the three were strangers; he had never seen Bowers before in his life till a few days ago. "We jest joined up t'ride together in case of some goddamn injun taken a shot at us."

The older man agreed. "If we'd knowed he was a wanted man we woulda done something else. We don't want no trouble with the law."

The deputy asked, "Bowers say anything to you what he was doin' out here?"

"Naw. We talked horses mostly. He seemed like a nice feller . . ."

"You never can be too goddamn careful," the deputy said darkly. "What you two doin' in Fairview?"

"Jest passing through," the taller man said.

The arrest was big news; both Pomfret and Morgan went to the jail to see for themselves and were only part of a like crowd. Bowers was sitting on a cot in the cell, clean shaven with his hair cut short and he did not greatly resemble the wanted poster. He glowered at them and did not answer the questions put to him.

But the deep cleft in his lip was unmistakable. The man was Bowers, right enough.

When they went back into the office the deputy told them that Bowers refused to talk to reporters and denied that he had done anything wrong.

The deputy said, "He told me his father'll sue the goddamn government because of them posters."

"That'll be interesting," Pomfret said, rubbing his

chin. "A trial will open up a huge basket of fish. We will welcome it."

Morgan had examined the jail. "Will this place hold him?"

The deputy was surprised. "Hell, we ain't never had a jailbreak!"

"Well, you never had Bowers in there, either."

CHAPTER TWELVE

Pomfret immediately wired his superiors that Gavin Bowers had been taken, and received orders to expect a detachment of special officers who would come for him and take him to Leavenworth Prison where a trial would be held when the government thought it had built a case against him.

It was a time to celebrate. Pomfret and Morgan visited the best restaurant in Fairview. It was a plain room with stucco walls that echoed every sound, ten sturdy tables with thin cloths and a heavy-set woman waitress who peered down her glasses at them.

"We'll have champagne," Pomfret said.

"We ain't got that, mister. I never seen any."

"Ummm. Do you have any wine at all?"

"They is some cooking sherry I think. I'll ask cook if you want."

"There must be something better than that!"

She shrugged. "I'll go see." She left them and reappeared in several moments with a bottle and set it on the table between them with a flourish. "It's the only one we got."

Pomfret said, "Will you have someone take the cork out please?"

She bit her lip. "Oh." She took the bottle away and came back in several minutes with it and two glasses.

Pomfret thanked her and poured into the glasses. He raised his and clinked it against Morgan's. "Here's to Bowers' hangman." He sipped the wine and made a terrible face.

"This tastes like ostrich piss!"

Morgan smiled. "How do you know?"

Pomfret grunted.

As they were ordering, Congressman Bates and Amanda came into the restaurant and were seated across the room from them. Morgan noted that Amanda espied him immediately and he winked at her.

The food was passable. What the west needs above all, Pomfret said, was chefs. There wasn't a decent cook within a thousand miles; all one had to do was order a meal in any eating house in any town to see he was correct.

That night Morgan went to Amanda's room again and gave the secret knock. She opened the door in her nightgown. "Come in quick!" He bolted the door behind him and she was in his arms. "I hoped you would come . . ."

"There's a reward out for me, you know. I have to be careful."

"I don't think you worry much about it. But maybe I'll collect it."

He kissed her hungrily. "I wish you wouldn't."

"I won't then, not until morning." She pulled at him. "Get undressed."

She watched him pull off his boots. "Why is father so upset with you and the general?"

"Oh — is he?"

"Oh yes. He says terrible things about General Pomfret."

Morgan shrugged. "I have no idea why." He pushed off his jeans and she wriggled close and snaked her hand into his crotch, giggling. He said, "But I wonder why your father is still on this train."

"You do? He says it's a vacation." She was working on the organ she found there. "I guess it's partly my fault, I begged him to take me somewhere . . . Ooooo, this is getting so big!"

He doffed his shirt and pushed into bed with her. She was right. It was big. He put it where it would best be employed. She slid her legs about him and moaned softly. "Oooo, push it in deep . . ."

It was the only gentlemanly thing to do. Though she was not terribly ladylike for the next several hours.

Pomfret was amused that Bates was unhappy with him but was curious about where Morgan had heard the gossip. Morgan merely shrugged, "Here and there." If he told the general about Amanda . . . !

They attended the fair much easier in their minds. There was great excitement when the President presented winners with their trophies on the platform — and no untoward happening.

There was a dance, advertised as Fairview's Gala

Affair, held in the evening. A crew of men had laid down a large board floor and built a small platform for the musicians and singers. The grounds were lighted by colored lanterns and it looked very attractive, especially with pretty girls in crisp dresses moving about in the arms of young men with slicked down hair.

Whiskey flowed from kegs set here and there and a number of persons staggered from one keg to the next, though some did not make it and rolled under wagons to sleep it off.

Morgan saw that Amanda attended the festivities with her dour father and danced, under his beady eye, with a few of the young men of the town. But, several of the town's politicians gathered about the congressman—how often did they have a chance to chat with an honest-to-God member of Congress? His attention wavered.

However, Morgan kept an eye on her and when one of the eager swains danced her to the edge of the floor then took her around behind a wagon where it was dark, Morgan started—then followed Bates who rushed from the circle of men and discovered Amanda with her skirts up and the young man about to enter paradise.

The young Colt was chased off and Bates took her back to the hotel at once, despite her bitter protests.

So her father knew about her. Morgan was not terribly surprised. There must have been dozens of incidents in the past. Bates must be very good at covering her tracks. Pomfret did not know about her.

Later in the hotel Pomfret informed him that the

presidential train would leave the next day about noon. He would stay in Fairview, however, and wait for the special agents who would take Bowers away.

"Shall I wait or go with the President?"

"You were hired to see to Bowers, and he's under lock and key." Pomfret rubbed his hands. "If the government has its way he'll never get out."

"Then I'm finished here?"

Pomfret smiled. "It would seem so. And I'm glad the job was concluded as quickly and well as it has. Will you go back to Toland now?"

"What about the charge against me?"

Pomfret nodded and got up to pace the room. "I'm sure we can arrange a pardon—if nothing else. After all, you're not guilty of anything."

"I *did* break out of jail."

"That can be explained. I've already started the wheels turning. You stay out of the public eye for a time and let me work it out."

A number of people, mostly local politicians, came to look at Gavin Bowers in his cell. He was a curiosity and the deputy sheriff who acted as town marshal basked in his reflected glory.

It was not allowed to talk to Bowers, but a few managed it when the deputy's attention was turned away.

The jail was in a stone building that was considerably larger than it looked from the street. The facade and the office walls were of cemented fieldstone but the jail area was planed boards, the roof was shingle.

There were seven cells, two very large. The larger ones usually contained drunks on weekends. When they sobered up they were released, often with small fines for disturbing the peace. A Justice of the Peace who lived nearby came to the jail each Monday morning for these rituals. His salary depended on the fines.

It was a good, stout jail, built by men who knew their trade, and at the moment was occupied by only one man, Bowers. There was little real crime in Fairview and the town had never had a hanging. If that became necessary the prisoner was transported to the county seat where there was a gallows.

Each day the deputy brought a tray of food for the prisoner. He received one meal a day and had been cautioned that if he wished to eat several meals he would have to divide the food himself. It meant he had only one hot meal but he was a criminal, after all. But if he had money he might bribe the deputy to bring him something else. Bowers had a bottle of brandy in the cell and plenty of tobacco.

When old Fred came to look at him, among a bunch of gawkers, he was able to slip Bowers a note.

Morgan moved into the room vacated by Amanda, for the several nights he would stay until he rode out for Toland.

There had been several men with Bowers when the train track was blown up, according to witnesses. He asked Pomfret, "Where were these men now?"

"If you mean they might effect a jailbreak, I assure you the jail is being manned day and night.

The office is stone and the door is three inch plank."

"The deputy has help?"

"He has one man in the office round the clock, besides himself."

"Is that sufficient?"

"Probably." Pomfret made a face. "At the first sign of trouble the door will be barred from the inside and if any shots are fired the citizens will come to the deputy's aid. Bowers is safe enough in his cell. He'll be put on the train in shackles and will ride in a baggage car outfitted with a cell." Pomfret smiled like a big cat after a hearty meal. "I think we've thought of everything."

"Yes, it sounds like it." Morgan scratched his chin absently. He asked, "Are there any of Bowers' friends — I mean the Company — in Fairview?"

"There may be, but no organized group. I think we have nothing to fear from them . . . at least not here. We'll switch cars before we get to a large town to avoid that sort of trouble. If they can't find us, they can't hurt us."

"Good idea."

Morgan went back to the small room and slid into bed, thinking about Amanda. How she had loved it, in this very bed! With her grouchy father next door, the idea adding to the spice. Well, a man got lucky now and then.

He drifted off to sleep — and woke to the explosion.

A loud series of *booms* and the concussion shook the building. Instantly he rolled out of bed and yanked on his jeans. Pushing his feet into boots, he grabbed his pistol and a shirt and ran out and down the stairs to the street.

People in various stages of dress spilled from buildings, "What happened? What was that?" Someone yelled and pointed; smoke was rising from the jail!

Morgan ran down the street. The jail! Explosion! Someone had dynamited Bowers out of jail! He knew it before he got there and looked at the damage. One side of the building was gone, torn out neatly, the steel bars standing in a row, starkly . . . and the jail was empty. As he looked, the deputy came staggering from the office, holding his head. He had been sleeping on a cot and the explosion had thrown him off it, banging him into the wall. He was dizzy and foggy . . . what happened? Somebody yelled for the doctor.

Morgan went closer. It looked as if the dynamiter had done a very careful job. He had used just enough powder to blow out the wall—and it looked as if Bowers had covered himself with the cot mattress—so he had known the explosion was coming!

The dynamiter had brought horses of course, and Bowers was probably laughing his head off by now as he rode into the prairie.

General Pomfret showed up, in a foul mood, realizing instantly what had happened. "We thought of everything but dynamite," he growled. "We should have known better."

There were a couple of small fires but they were quickly put out. No one would use the jail for a while. Bowers' friends had seen to that. The doctor came and examined the deputy, putting a bandage on his head. The stone office was largely untouched and he went back to lie on the cot, a very unhappy man.

Pomfret routed out the telegrapher and sent a message east to report that Bowers had escaped. It was a bad night all around.

In the morning the telegraph was busy. The escape was even bigger news than the arrest. Everyone speculated on what Bowers' next move would be. Someone in Washington had let the cat out of the bag about the man and his Cause. Every newspaper picked it up and there were lurid stories about assassinations . . .

However, the President issued a statement saying he was afraid of no bandit and low-life and intended to continue his tour despite all that had happened. He was generally applauded for his courage.

Pomfret obtained tickets on the next train for them and Morgan packed his few things and they went to the depot. The game wasn't over after all.

They were barely on the train when the candy butcher came through and Pomfret bought the latest daily from the east. He had a cigar going and nearly dropped it when he opened the paper and said, "Oh, my God!"

His staring eyes met Morgan's. "Look at this!"

Shel was startled to see the lurid illustration, a wild-looking gunman with two pistols holding off a mob of raging people! It was done in reds and blacks with streaks of yellow, as garish as possible. The caption read: SHELTER MORGAN DEFENDS THE PRESIDENT IN THE WILD WEST!

"Holy Christ!" Morgan said in disbelief. "Who made that up?"

The story had a by-line: Harry Clemens.

Shel Morgan read down the column quickly. The story stated the notorious gunman, Shelter Morgan, had been hired to defend the President against brigands and Indians—or in fact any person wishing him harm. The west, said the article, was full of unsavory characters.

The President and his party were traveling the far west and had already barely escaped death at the hands of a mad dynamiter who had luckily been driven off by Shelter Morgan's guns.

The story went on to say that Gavin Bowers, one of the chief proponents of a secret and powerful ex-Copperhead organization had been jailed in the little town of Fairview—but had escaped.

Shelter Morgan, the paper said, was on his trail.

General Pomfret's face was pale as he read the preposterous words. "Someone has made all this up out of the whole cloth! There's hardly a word of truth in it! Can this Harry Clemens be a real person?"

"It says he's a reporter."

Pomfret shook the paper. "Where does he get such imaginative information!?"

"He makes it up." Morgan shook his head, frowning at the illustration. It looked nothing like him, thank the gods.

"This means all secrecy is gone," Pomfret said heavily. He glanced around as if expecting to see Clemens in the corner of the room with his notepad. "Someone on this train has obviously been selling information to the press."

"And Harry Clemens has put two and two together to make seven."

"Yes . . ."

They were in one of the tiny Pullman rooms and Morgan leaned on the arm of the chair and stared at passing scenery. It *was* annoying as hell.

"It's one thing," Pomfret said in a growling voice, "to collect the news, and quite another to fabricate it! The rise of yellow journalism in this country is a damned disgrace! I hope Congress will do something about it."

"Is there anything that can be done about it?"

The general let out his breath and sighed deeply. "Maybe not—free speech and all. But someone is going to sue one of these yellow rags one day and a jury is going to award a bundle! Mark my words." He wadded up the paper and tossed it away.

Morgan rubbed his chin. "With all the talk of assassination, will the President cut the tour short and go back to Washington?"

Pomfret made a face. "Oh, I don't think so. It's not good politics to let the nation see you turn tail, to show them you're afraid. No, I predict he'll issue a statement saying he will not be cowed by criminals and will continue the tour no matter what."

"I think you're right."

Pomfret was silent a moment, then said, "But I'd like to kick Harry Clemens—whoever he is—off the train, personally."

The President's car was on a siding when they

reached Galton the next day. Galton was the largest town in the area and a Bill show was playing in the nearby fields. It was advertised in huge red letters edged with gold as the most famous Wild West Show in the world! The colorful posters showed a train robbery, charging Indians and gallant cowboys rescuing beautifully coiffed maidens from scalping knives.

"The most famous show in the land?" Pomfret said, chuckling. "They can say that perhaps because Buffalo Bill Cody's show is in Europe."

"Maybe Harry Clemens writes their advertising material," Morgan suggested.

Pomfret laughed. "I wouldn't be surprised."

Even with General Pomfret's name and political pull they were able to obtain only one ordinary room in a second class hotel. But the hotel did supply another bed in the room and they settled in. Morgan bought himself a bath and a shave by a real barber, invested in a new shirt and began to feel downright civilized. He was not terribly surprised to discover that Amanda and her father were staying in the best hotel, a block down the street. The congressman apparently had better pull than the general.

But where there was Congressman Bates, could Gavin Bowers be far behind?

He met Amanda as she was coming out of the general store and her eyes lit up on seeing him. She hurried to join him, "Shel! How good to see you!"

"Hello, Amanda."

She took his arm. "We thought—well, Papa thought, that we'd left you behind. What happened?"

"The prisoner escaped. You hadn't heard? Bowers broke out of jail."

"No, I hadn't heard." She smiled sweetly. "I seldom read the papers, you know." She squeezed his arm. Her voice was soft and wheedling. "Why don't you come back to the hotel with me?"

"Where's your father?"

"I've no idea. He goes out seeing people you know. All the mayors and officials . . . Politics, he says. He won't be at the hotel."

He thought about it. She did look delicious in the gentle sunlight. "There's a restaurant in the hotel, isn't there?"

"Yes . . ."

"Well, let's have lunch then."

"Oh, I'd love to." She giggled and they turned to walk. "I saw the most exciting show last night—all those Indians. Are they really wild?"

"I guess some are."

"It was terribly noisy—and dusty. So much shooting! My clothes smelled of gunpowder afterward."

He noticed people watching them as they walked along the street together, with her clinging to his arm. It felt good to be with a pretty girl.

They went up the steps to the hotel. A gilded sign pointed the way to the restaurant. Morgan doffed his hat and followed her through the wide waiting room.

A clerk appeared suddenly, hurrying from the desk. "Miss Bates . . ."

She halted, brows raised.

"There's a letter for you." The clerk handed it over with a little bow.

"Thank you." She gave him a smile and turned the letter over and over in her hand as if wondering where it came from.

It was addressed to her and on the back was a name: Harry Clemens.

CHAPTER Thirteen

They were seated at a table before he said, "You know the reporter, Harry Clemens?"

She batted her eyes at him. "Well, I hardly know him . . . he introduced himself a few weeks ago. I'm sure he wanted to interview father. I don't know if he did or not."

"Amanda—did you mention my name to him?"

She colored prettily. "Oh, Shel—you *are* famous, you know."

"You did talk to him then."

"Oh, we talked, yes. It seems to me he did most of the talking."

"You talked about me?"

She reached across and squeezed his arm. "Whatever are you asking all these questions for?"

He sighed. So it had been Amanda who had given the reporter his wild ideas. She was the one who had wanted to know how many men he had killed. What a mad image of him she must have in her foolish little head! He said finally, "I was just curious, that's all."

They ordered lunch, cold beef sandwiches and coffee, then Amanda went up to her room and he followed in several minutes. She left the door ajar and he slipped in and bolted it.

She had read the letter and left it on a chest of drawers and was naked except for a thin little nightie. Grinning, she came and helped him undress, especially giving her attention to his pants buttons where there was a tenting effect. He got his boots off and managed to get the jeans off though she entangled herself in his arms, keeping a stranglehold on his shaft. He got her onto the bed at last and stripped off the nightie.

The bed squeaked a bit and he hoped it could not be heard in the hallway; Amanda seemed not to care. She was more wanton than he'd ever seen her, and he found himself wondering if Harry Clemens had occupied this same space. But she gave him little time for daydreaming . . . until at last she seemed sated and relaxed in his arms.

When she drifted off to sleep, he slid off the bed and began to dress. With his boots on, he picked up the letter. Clemens *had* been to bed with her, and wanted a repeat. Well, Morgan didn't blame him. He put the letter down and finished dressing.

She woke when he pulled a blanket over her, put her arms up and tried to pull him down, but he kissed her and slipped out of the room.

He debated telling Pomfret where the leak had come from, then decided against it. Pomfret might worm the truth out of him, and he didn't want to upset the general's pristine picture of Amanda.

He went to see the Bill show that evening. It was

held in a racetrack area where there were already spectators' benches. Most towns had racetracks, it being a very popular sport and a method of betting to boot.

A sort of grandstand had been erected for the presidential party. It was heavy with banners and flags and the President was there, beaming and talking to aides and friends. Morgan wondered if Congressman Bates was among them, smiling to the President and yet planning to dispatch him.

How could he bring down the man? He would have to scrape together incontrovertible evidence. He would almost have to catch Bates in the act of pulling a trigger. Not likely.

The show was like all other wild west shows he had seen, much shooting, yelling and racing around the oval track; there was a stage holdup and a group of red Indians whooping and hollering. And when it was over at last he filed out with the others and walked back to the small hotel to find Pomfret up and writing his endless letters.

Gavin Bowers was not a man to give up easily; he was also a man to hold a grudge. There had been saloon talk in Fairview, duly reported to him by old Fred, that General Pomfret was one of the men responsible for putting him in jail—whether this was true or not, Bowers believed it. Someone had to be. It was known that Pomfret traveled with the President.

And now that the Harry Clemens story had been given wide circulation, he knew that Shelter Morgan was also among that party. Morgan was a man far more to be feared than Pomfret. But Pomfret was highly placed. His passing would leave a large void. Bowers thought about Pomfret's passing a good deal. It shouldn't be too difficult to get to him.

According to the notices posted outside every telegraph office, the President was at Galton. Bowers, Jordan and old Fred bought tickets on the next train and boarded separately.

Pomfret was proved right. The President issued a statement saying the threats of criminals would never deter him from his duty and would not cause him to change one single aspect of his grand tour.

However, it did. The guard pattern was tightened and Colonel Hobby considered hiring several Pinkerton detectives. He discussed the matter by wire with his superiors in the War Department and it was finally decided to wait and see.

The President made only a few speeches to selected groups at Galton, especially those of his own party as he met men who were running for local office. Then the presidential cars were hooked to the next engine and the tour went on.

This train was very long: an engine, dining car, six passenger cars, two baggage cars and a caboose. The President's car, one of the six, was just before the diner, and was closed off from the diner. The President's food was prepared by his own chef on the long car in a tiny kitchen.

There were several more stops, one for taking on water and one for a short speech from a wagon. A hundred or more people were gathered in buggies and wagons and the President would not disappoint them. Though Colonel Hobby wrung his hands, the President climbed onto a wagon bed and delivered the speech.

Morgan roamed through the crowd, seeing nothing untoward. Another large group of people stood beneath the President's wagon, listening. Congressman Bates, with his usual scowl, and Amanda were there. She kept turning her head to look at Morgan and Bates yanked her arm several times. General Pomfret prowled the edge of the crowd, chewing a cigar, eyeing the troopers which Colonel Hobby distributed about the area.

But the speech concluded and the President climbed down to enthusiastic applause and went back to his private car to receive several officials of the town.

When he joined Pomfret the general said, "I don't like it. Too calm. Too calm."

"You don't like it either way, calm or noisy!"

Pomfret looked at him. "Hmmmm." He looked at the cigar, decided it was finished and tossed it away.

Morgan said, "This is a bad spot to kill a man and get away with it."

"What?"

Morgan indicated the undulating prairie. "Where would he hide? Hobby's men would have him inside an hour."

Pomfret sighed. "There's that, I suppose. But by your reckoning our next stop should keep us up nights."

Morgan nodded. The next stop was Newmark

City, a settlement of probably six to eight thousand souls alongside the Badger River. It was a center of stagecoach lines and the railroad had come to it only recently.

"There's an active Company there," Pomfret said, patting his breast pocket for another cigar. "We're told the leader is a name named Simon Pake. We've asked the police in Newmark to arrest and hold him on any charge at all, but he can't be found."

"Will there be a parade?"

The general bit off the end of the cigar. "There's a weather report that it may rain. That may save us — but unless it does, yes, there's a parade scheduled. I'm told they even have some elephants in the city. There's a zoo of sorts."

"I've never seen an elephant," Morgan said with interest.

"Well, you may."

It took a day to reach Newmark and the train arrived about dusk, rattling into a large covered station with a light rain pattering down. The presidential party was taken at once to a hotel where the city officials were presented. Pomfret and Morgan walked a block in the rain to a moderate hotel. They had a good supper in the restaurant next door and retired early.

The next morning as Morgan followed Pomfret out of the hotel, he looked up as the puff of smoke blossomed from a window across the street. The shot was a flat report and Pomfret grunted suddenly and was flung back into Morgan's arms.

Morgan laid the big man down easily and snaked out his pistol — but there was no further shot. It had come from the second window on the third floor; the window was open, the curtain moving in the slight breeze.

He looked down at Pomfret. "It's my arm," the general said. He was holding his shoulder. Several men ran from the hotel and paused by Pomfret. Morgan said, "Take care of him."

He ran across the street. There was a line of stores; the windows upstairs were probably living quarters and there was a stairway to the right. He went up it three at a time. Had the shot been meant for Pomfret or for him? There was a hall at the top of the stairs. He ran down it to the left where there were two doors. The first was slightly ajar.

He drew the hammer of the pistol back and pushed the door wide open. He peered into the room, an ordinary sitting room that had a vaguely vacant look about it. He stepped inside, the revolver ready. There was a faint smell of powder in the air. There was a bedroom attached and no one in the rooms. He hurried back to the door and ran down the hall to the end, finding an ell. As he came around the corner there was a shot and plaster sprayed from the wall just over his head. Someone had fired from the bottom of the steps.

The steps were dark as someone slammed the door at the bottom. He ran down, opened the door and pressed himself to the wall. There was another shot, too quick, and Morgan fired back at the smoke. It came from a fence. He put three shots through the board fence, then ran across a littered yard. He scrambled over the fence and found himself in an alley.

There was no one in sight.

He looked for tracks but the ground was hard, despite the rain. The sniper might have gone in any direction. He walked along the alley in each direction, but saw no one.

He gave up the search and went back to the hotel, reloading the pistol. Pomfret had been carried inside and a doctor had come, had cut off the shirt and was bandaging the wound.

Morgan identified himself and the doctor said, "It broke the humerus, the bone of the upper arm. I've set it and splinted it and he'll be fine. It'll be very uncomfortable for a bit . . . Are you traveling?"

"Not for a few days."

"Then bring him around to see me in a day or so." He gave Morgan a card.

Pomfret was grumpy, more annoyed at the inconvenience than anything else, Morgan thought. It was the left arm. If the sniper had aimed a fraction to the right, Pomfret would be a memory.

When they went up to Pomfret's room he asked, "Did you see him?"

"The sniper? No, he got away clean. He had it well planned. Did the doctor give you something for the pain?"

The general held up a bottle. "I'll take some more in an hour or so."

"I'll go down and tell the desk we don't want to see any reporters."

Pomfret nodded. "Good idea. Was he shooting at me or at you?"

"Probably at you." Morgan went to the door and paused, then he went to his pack and took out the pistol he'd taken from the man in Fairview who had tried to turn him in for the reward. He gave it to Pomfret. "Here, you'd better carry this."

"Thanks." Pomfret examined it and laid it on the table beside him.

Morgan went downstairs to the clerk.

CHAPTER FOURTEEN

The President sent one of his aides to see Pomfret on hearing the news of the shooting. "The boss is worried about you," he told Pomfret. "He doesn't want you leaning up against any bullets."

"Tell him I feel exactly the same way," the general said. "The doctor tells me I'll be good as new in a few weeks."

When the aide had gone he said to Morgan, "Was this Gavin Bowers' doing, d'you think?"

"I don't know who else."

"Maybe it's frustration."

"If so, he may get careless."

He quickly discovered that Congressman Rufus Bates was staying in a hotel near that of the President. He took up station outside the hotel, determined to follow Bates, hoping the man would lead him to Bowers.

It was a tiresome vigil; Bates did not show himself until late in the afternoon. When he came out finally he was alone, walking fast with only a glance around him. At the first corner he climbed into a cab and Morgan was hard put to find one for himself before Bates was out of sight.

Bates led him into a market section where heavy wagons loaded with farm produce rumbled along cobblestones, where warehouses stood in rows and men were busy as ants loading and unloading boxes and bales. There was considerable traffic and Morgan urged his driver to get closer.

At one point, as Bates' cab was stalled allowing a four horse team to pass, a man came out of the crowd and jumped into the Congressman's cab. Morgan got only a quick view of him, slight and tall, poorly dressed.

Bates' cab turned immediately and worked out of the district, onto a wide street. Morgan had to hang far back. Bates went a mile or more, then turned off the street. When Morgan followed he saw Bates and the other man climb out of the cab and hurry into a shabby building, one of a line of such.

Morgan went on past, noting the building. It had a small sign on the front: Grover Pake Construction.

What had Pomfret said . . . The Company leader was a man named Simon Pake! This must be a relative. He paid off the cabbie and walked back to the street to find a place from which he could keep the front of the building in view and not be seen himself. Was Gavin Bowers inside? Probably.

He ought to send a message to Pomfret and have him get Colonel Hobby to surround the building. But if he left, they might all come out and disappear.

Several hours passed. When it was good and dark

he walked to the building to examine it closer. There was a rutted driveway on the right, beside a high board fence. He went down the drive with the pistol in his hand, but met no one. The building was two stories, and when he got to the back, could see a light in one of the upper rooms.

The fence continued around the property. In the back were large bins containing building materials; there were two huge wains, a smaller wagon and a row of privies. Near the privies was a hitchrack and four saddled horses.

He tried the rear door, finding it locked. There was a basement door, also locked. So were the ground floor windows.

There was nothing more he could do here. He went back to the main street and started walking.

Frank Willis sat in a cafe with a newspaper spread out on the table before him. He looked at an illustration of an evil-looking man with two pistols, holding a mob at bay. The caption said it was Shelter Morgan who was guarding the President on his tour.

So that was where Morgan had gone.

The newspaper printed the President's itinerary, with a map. Frank smiled to himself. Enough time had gone by so that Morgan had undoubtedly forgotten Keno Willis and would not be on his guard. It should be possible to get close to him to put a bullet where it would do the most good — or harm, as the case might be.

He left the newspaper on the table and walked to

the stage office and bought a ticket for Newmark City.

When Shel Morgan got back to the hotel Pomfret was sitting up, grumbling and half drunk, a bottle of whiskey at his elbow. "Kills the pain," he said as Morgan eyed the bottle.

"I thought the doctor gave you something."

"He did, but it makes me sleepy. Where you been?"

"I followed Rufus Bates." He told Pomfret what he'd seen and what he suspected. "They're making more plans. Bet my saddle."

"You prob'ly right." Pomfret was slurring his words a bit. He eased himself in the chair. "While you's gone, I hadda talk with Hobby." He reached for a glass and sipped the brown liquor. "President's gonna speak at the theater tomorra night."

"Which theater?"

"27th Street Theater. Is for th' local veteran's club — forget the name. President was a gen'ral in the war, you know. Wounded four times. Didju know that?"

Morgan shook his head.

"Two horses shot under 'im." Pomfret finished the liquid and frowned at the glass. "Brave man." He sighed. "Lotsa brave men, both sides. Goddamn brave men." There were tears in Pomfret's eyes.

"Can you sleep in the bed?"

"I dunno. Haven't tried it. Didja know I met Gen'ral Lee one time?"

Morgan was astonished. "You met Bob Lee?"

"Yus I did. Damn right. Fine man, Shel. We never had anybody could wear 'is boots." He shook his head. "Nobody. Maybe nobody in the whole worl' like Gen'ral Lee. Got to admit it." He looked up blearily. "What I talking about?"

"You were telling me the President is going to speak at the 27th Street Theater."

"Yus. Tomorra night." Pomfret picked up the bottle and tried to pour into the glass. Morgan took it out of his hand and poured the glass a third full.

"Thanks." Pomfret took a gulp. "Keeps the pain away," he explained again. He shook his head. "Don' get shot, Shel."

"I'll try not to." He smiled as Pomfret's head fell and he closed his eyes. The general's face showed more lines than he'd seen in it before. Getting shot was more than he really needed.

Pomfret looked comfortable in the big chair. Morgan debated trying to move him to the bed. It might hurt him more than if he just let him sleep here. Pomfret was a big man. He decided to leave him be.

But he ought to look at the theater.

He slept in the same room with Pomfret, but the other hardly moved during the night. But he woke with a terrible head and a miserable taste in his mouth. Morgan dressed and got out while Pomfret grumbled and growled. The wound was probably more annoyance the second day. He would take the general to see the doctor tomorrow.

He had breakfast of eggs and bacon then inquired the way to the theater. He took a horse cab and arrived quickly; it was only a short distance from the hotel. The theater was in an old building, brick, wrought iron decorations and polished wood. A crew of men was busy cleaning and scrubbing, preparing for the President's visit.

Colonel Hobby was there also, looking to the security arrangements. Morgan was taken to him when he asked entrance and Hobby nodded. "Hello, Morgan. Glad to see you. How's the general?"

"Grumpy as hell."

Hobby grinned. "I don't doubt it. I hear his upper arm bone was broken."

"Yes."

"Well then, he's got a right to howl a bit I'd say. I would too. Have you come to see what we're doing?"

"I'd like to — with your permission."

"Of course."

The colonel was in uniform, blue shirt and shining black boots, with a broad yellow stripe down each leg, cavalry colors. He was wearing a cream colored hat, broad brimmed, with a silver eagle on the front. Hobby was rather a dandy, Morgan thought.

They walked into the theater. It seated about five hundred, Hobby said. But when the President spoke there would be easily another hundred standing.

"I'd like to search every person entering," Hobby said, "but they won't let me. However, I'll have experts watching and we'll pull anyone out of line who looks suspicious."

Morgan gazed at the rows of empty seats, smelling the familiar odors. The ceiling was flat, painted a dark color. There was a broad balcony and as he looked at it, Hobby remarked, "No place for anyone to hide up there. I'll have six men stationed, three on each side."

"What about backstage?"

The colonel frowned. "There're lots of nooks and crannies there. About all I can do is have men moving constantly, looking at everything and everybody. the curtain will be right behind the President when he speaks. I'll put three men there, behind the curtain of course. So no one can get close."

It seemed that Hobby had thought of everything.

There was a door at the side of the theater and as he glanced toward it, Hobby said in explanation, "There's an alley outside that leads to the street. The door will be closed and bolted during the speech, but afterward we'll open it as another exit."

One of his officers called Hobby away then, and Morgan went out to the alley. There was a fire escape on the side of the building, with a landing at each floor. It was iron and looked very solid. He noted that the steps also continued up from the last floor, to the roof. He frowned at those stairs. What could someone do from the roof?

He mounted the iron steps as a group of troopers eyed him. He went all the way up to the roof, which was domed. He walked around it, seeing nothing out of the way. The ceiling inside was flat, so there was a space inside the dome. But he could find no way in.

On the side of the building away from the fire escape was another roof, probably ten feet lower than where he stood. It was flat, with vent pipes sticking up, and several chimneys . . .

He went back and climbed down to the ground.

There would be a dinner first, the colonel told him, then the President would come here for the speech. Immediately after, he would return to the hotel, which should be about midnight.

Morgan went out to the street, thinking about the dome. If someone got into it, he might easily chop a hole in the ceiling, enough to push a rifle barrel through . . .

But he had looked carefully at the tarred roof and seen nothing out of the way. Was it possible for a clever workman to camouflage an opening? The thought made him very uneasy. He went back inside the theater to find Colonel Hobby.

CHAPTER FIFTEEN

Hobby was conferring with two officers and three men in plainclothes; they looked as if they might be policemen. Morgan waited, standing to one side and after a bit Hobby came over to him. "Did you look the place over?"

"Yes. I'm wondering about the roof. There's a space between the ceiling and the outside roof."

"Yes. I had it investigated. There's nothing in it but support posts and the like."

"Couldn't a man get in there?"

Hobby nodded. "There's room almost to stand up in the center, but how would he get in without making a noise?"

Morgan smiled. "I dunno, but it makes me nervous."

The West Pointer glanced at the ceiling. "All right, say he got in . . . somehow. He'd have to have a lantern to see his way, because if he missed a step he'd come crashing down through the plaster. If he had a lantern and somehow made a hole in the ceiling to shoot by—we'd be sure to see the light."

Morgan rubbed his chin. The colonel made it sound as if it were impossible. But the man they were taking precautions against was wily and clever. He had evaded them thus far—except for the brief time in jail, and his exit from *that* had been spectacular.

Thinking of dynamite made him shudder. But certainly Hobby had searched the area under the stage ... What a story if the President should be blown sky high!

He told Colonel Hobby then of the construction building and how he'd followed Congressman Bates there.

"Did you see anyone else?"

"No, Bates went in the door as if he had a key. But there were four saddled horses behind the building. I assumed it was a meeting place."

Hobby nodded solemnly. "Should we surround it or watch it? If we went in and found Bates not there—" He shrugged. "You say the sign read Pake Construction? Even if we found Bates there, what could we prove—unless we found papers that were criminal evidence."

Morgan smiled again. "Well, you know about it now."

"Thanks."

When he got back to the hotel, Pomfret was asleep on the bed, half dressed. A tumbler of water and the bottle the doctor had given him was on the bedside table. Morgan eased off the big man's shoes and drew a blanket up over him.

Pomfret had several newspapers strewn on the

floor by the bed. Morgan picked them up and sat by a window trying to read. But the words kept blurring. All he could think about was that domed roof. A man *could* get into it . . . couldn't he? Hobby was too cocksure. If a man got into the dome, with a lantern to show the way, what was to prevent him from putting his foot through the ceiling—Hobby had said it was easily possible—and fire a six gun at the President—or a shotgun! The foot through the ceiling would make a racket, and so would the gun! So what difference? The President would be dead.

And the assassin might easily scuttle back through his hole in the roof and get away across the roof of the next building before guards could climb up to stop him.

It *could* be done!

General Pomfret woke in the late afternoon, irritable because the arm was paining him. He drank a huge gulp of whiskey and settled himself in the big chair, asking Morgan to get him the latest newspaper. He did not feel like attending the speech that night, he said; he did not feel like doing anything at all but sitting in the damned chair.

Morgan went downstairs and bought a *Harper's* and the late edition of the *Democrat* and took them back upstairs. "Are you going to eat anything tonight?"

Pomfret shook his head. "Not hungry. Maybe later." He poured a generous amount of whiskey into the glass and sipped it.

"Is there anything I can do for you?"

Pomfret growled. "Stop mothering me."

Morgan nodded and slipped out quickly. The arm must hurt like blue blazes. He would take Pomfret to see the doctor in the morning.

Amanda was in the lobby of the hotel when he went downstairs again. He managed to avoid her; she was with another woman, standing by the front window, chatting. He went along the street to a restaurant and had supper alone, still worrying the domed roof, like a dog with a bone, he thought. Should he insist that Colonel Hobby take some action about it? If he did, he might get nowhere. After all, Hobby was in charge and might resent his interference.

Of course if he were right and it happened the way he feared it might, Hobby would look bad . . . and might even be cashiered for ignoring good advice. But then Hobby was not stupid. Maybe he would have men on the roof to guard against what Morgan feared. Maybe.

Morgan was at the theater well before the President was scheduled to arrive. He walked the streets restlessly noting that near the theater were many stores that had living quarters on the second floor. If a man got on the roof of any one of them he could easily make his way across to the theater roof, if he had a small ladder.

Crowds began to gather about the theater, almost closing off the street. A dozen or more uniformed policemen tried to keep people on the sidewalks to allow carriages to deposit guests and depart. Morgan worked his way into the alley and was relieved to see that Hobby had stationed men on the theater roof. Possibly he had begun to worry about that possibility also. He was fairly smart, for a Yankee.

Morgan had no desire at all to enter the theater. The President was likely to make one of the half dozen speeches he had already heard, so he stationed himself outside to watch the faces of those going in.

He saw no one who looked like Gavin Bowers. But Congressman Bates and Amanda were there, with Amanda's eyes lighting up as she saw him. He gave her a smile and then she was gone, pushed along by the crowd.

The front of the theater was well lighted by hanging lanterns and the police had gotten the crowd in hand and had strung ropes to keep people back out of the way of the horses.

There was rising excitement when the presidential coach appeared. It was black with red trim and had two American flags prominent on top where the coachman sat. There was a troop of cavalry with it, men in front and rear. The crowd surged forward as the carriage clattered in and stopped. The horsemen milled about and a footman jumped down and opened the door, letting down the iron steps. Police pushed the crowd back and the President stepped down. He was wearing a black cloak and a top hat and, Morgan thought, looked rather odd. There was something about him . . .

He was with two other men, the First Lady was not in the carriage.

And then it came. Morgan was looking almost directly at the window when he saw the blossom of smoke. It came from across the street and the sound of the shot echoed as he saw the President stumble. The .44 Colt was in his hand instantly and he sent five shots into the window as fast as he could pull the trigger.

A great shout went up from the crowd, women screamed and Morgan was into the street, running for the row of buildings on the far side. Seeing the pistol in his hand, the crowd parted and he ran along the row of stores looking for a way up. A half dozen police were running with him and one shouted. They piled into the stairway and clattered up to a hall . . . and halted.

In the hallway, by the measly light of a gas lamp, was the body of a man. He was half in and half out of a doorway. There was a rifle on the floor behind him.

Morgan knelt and turned him over. No pulse. There were at least three shots in his chest—it was a pulp.

"Dead," someone said. "The sonofabitch got what he deserved."

A sergeant took charge and Morgan went downstairs, holstering the pistol. He had got the assassin—but the President was dead. He was certain of it.

CHAPTER SIXTEEN

The President had been immediately carried into the theater, into a private room. Morgan pushed into the foyer with people jabbering excitedly all around him. Colonel Hobby caught his eye and beckoned and Morgan made his way to him. Hobby said, "This way."

He led him into a hall, roped off with troopers standing guard. He was in an office with a connecting room. Through the open door he could see the President, standing, apparently unhurt!

Colonel Hobby said, "We put a bulletproof shield around him, just in case—and as you saw, it was needed."

Morgan stared. "But that's not the President!"

"That's right." Hobby grinned at him. "We used a double, a very brave volunteer."

So that was why he had thought the President looked odd! He walked into the next room with Hobby. The volunteer had shed the steel shield, which had taken a well-aimed shot squarely in the back. He was a man who resembled the President and had fooled everyone in the lamplight, with top hat and high collared cloak.

And as he looked, the President came into the room, smiling. He had come in through the alley entrance, Hobby said quietly. Mr. Hayes shook hands with the volunteer and thanked him for his courage. Then he came to Shel Morgan.

"I understand you are the man who shot down the assassin."

"Yes sir," Morgan said.

"You are Shelter Morgan . . ."

"Yes sir."

"I thank you for your good aim, sir. And how is General Pomfret?"

"He is grumpy, sir. The arm pains him a good deal."

The President shook his head. "I expect it does. Please give him my very best regards. I expect to see him soon."

"I will, sir."

"I have signed a pardon for you, Mr. Morgan—wait, I believe I should call you Colonel Morgan." He smiled. "Pomfret has explained the matter of the jailbreak. The pardon will cover it."

"Thank you, sir."

The President smiled and moved away. Well, that was a relief. Pomfret had said he would do something . . .

When the President left to go backstage, Morgan spoke to Hobby. "Why didn't you tell me you had a double?"

"I told as few as possible. Only five of us knew,

not counting the President himself." Hobby smiled. "If you had known, you might not have been where you were, to shoot the damned sniper."

Morgan sighed. "Well, it worked out. Do you know the identity of the man?"

"Not yet. The police will track that down for us. But I congratulate you on some fine shooting."

The entire matter of the shooting was hushed up. The President wanted no scare headlines. A number of people had seen what they thought was the President being shot in front of the theater, but a few moments later, they saw him on the stage obviously in the best of health, delivering a long energetic speech.

This was confusing to some, especially when no mention was made of the shooting in the local newspapers. And since it was apparent to all that the President was unharmed the matter was swept under the rug.

Colonel Hobby held a quiet news conference of reporters and explained the reasons for the hush up. He feared that someone whose reason was less than normal might attempt a copycat killing.

No one wanted to see the chief executive murdered and the reporters readily agreed to kill the stories.

Pomfret was astonished at Colonel Hobby's subterfuge and laughed heartily when Morgan explained it all to him. "That boy has imagination!" he exclaimed. "It was exactly the right thing to do under the circumstances. I must send him my congratulations."

Morgan helped him dress and they went downstairs and got into a cab for the drive to the doctor's office. He was still in considerable pain, Pomfret said, as the doctor took off the bandages and examined the wound.

"It is knitting nicely," the doctor told him. "The pain will lessen, but do not try to be active."

In the horse cab on the way back, Pomfret growled, "Do not try to be active." He snorted. "What does that man expect of me?"

Morgan helped the general pack, and in the morning the presidential party left on the train and when they met Rufus Bates in the diner much later, the congressman seemed even more grumpy.

Amanda squeezed Morgan's hand as he passed her and her father in the aisle. There was no chance to see her alone.

Colonel Hobby received a wire at the first stop. The police had identified the assassin as a man named Jordan Larson an ex-convict with a long record. He was known to be a member of a Company and was probably one of the leaders.

Hobby said to Morgan, "That means he was undoubtedly working under Gavin Bowers."

"Probably. I'm only sorry it wasn't Bowers in that window."

"Me too," Hobby said with feeling.

"Bowers has been very energetic in his attempts on the President — will he continue?"

Hobby shrugged. "Don't ask me what's in his mind, but remember he's a fanatic. He doesn't think like you or me. I'm afraid nothing will stop him from trying — until we put a bullet into him."

"And we have to find him first."

"That's right."

As the train left Newmark City and entered the rolling prairie, a group of horsemen approached the speeding engine and began to fire on it. Stray shots smashed several windows and people ducked down, sprawling in the aisles while the troopers returned the fire and one horse was seen to stumble and fall.

The train soon outdistanced the horsemen and in a short time it was announced that no one had been hurt. Pomfret thought it was probably an expression of frustration on the part of some Company members.

"Colonel Hobby outfoxed 'em and they're mad about it."

The next two days were uneventful. Pomfret's arm was giving him less trouble; he went about with it securely fastened in a sling and some of his good humor returned. On the third day he conferred with Colonel Hobby and was closeted with the President for more than an hour.

When he returned to the compartment he said, "We're cutting a week — well, the President is cutting a week off the tour. It seems that foreign affairs are worrying him as well as some strikes. He thinks he ought to get back to the White House."

"So what does that mean?"

"It means some first class worry for Colonel Hobby. When we reach Louiston this evening we'll have to leave the train and go across country to Tamarind by stagecoach."

Morgan rubbed his chin. "How many know about this?"

Pomfret counted on his fingers. "Six people. Now seven, with you."

"Well, it may not be that bad. We're positive Bowers is not on this train . . ."

"But Rufus Bates is."

"But how would Bates get word to Gavin Bowers? I suggest you tell Colonel Hobby to post troopers at the telegraph office when we reach Louiston—just in case."

Pomfret fished out a cigar and rolled it in his fingers. "Good idea. But the best thing is secrecy. What Bowers doesn't know can't help him. If we're lucky we'll transfer everybody to the coaches and be off before Bowers knows about it. There is no way in the world he could expect it."

Morgan nodded. "How far is Tamarind?"

"About two days' ride I think. We'll go across country to the railroad and maybe lose him in the dust."

Louiston was a good sized town situated near a line of hills, the center of several intersecting roads. The brick depot was new and pristine, having recently replaced the wooden one which had burned down. The passenger cars were shunted to a siding and the members of the presidential party were then told they would be boarding the stagecoaches in the morning for the overland ride to Tamarind. There was considerable grumbling. Congressman Bates demanded a hearing with the President but was refused.

When he went to the telegraph office he was

refused there also by a corporal and two troopers. "Nobody sends no wires, sir."

"By whose orders!?"

"Colonel Hobby, sir. You got to talk to him."

Bates stumped off, swearing under his breath.

The transfer to stagecoaches entailed a considerable amount of juggling and making do. Louiston was a stage center, it being the largest town in hundreds of miles, and also a connecting point with the railroad. But the stage yard had only four coaches available; they'd had no advance notice. There were several mud wagons but they were much less comfortable on a journey—not that the Concords were models of comfort.

Colonel Hobby's troopers were cavalry, dismounted. They had no horses with them. The local livery could furnish no more than eighteen horses, and some of them were not particularly cavalry standard.

The presidential party would have to be pared down, as would the troopers. Colonel Hobby, his lieutenants and the President's aides worked long hours revising and reorganizing but they were not ready by the next morning; it would all take another day. The livery had sent out calls and six more horses were gathered in, and finally the four available coaches were sorted out. The Concords could carry 15 passengers in a pinch but for the journey to Tamarind it was decided that no more than six inside and one on top would do. The middle bench was taken out of each of them. The remainder of the party would travel in mud wagons or wait until later.

Hobby had thirty troopers; a few would have to

travel in the wagons with baggage, and by midday of the following day they were all ready, and at Hobby's order the little procession moved out.

General Pomfret was in the second coach with Morgan on the box in shotgun position beside the driver, glad to be off the train.

The weather was holding fair with high, streaky clouds and very little wind. The road curled around the hills and went straight as a gunshot across the desert till it disappeared into the ground haze. Dust from the wagons' wheels drifted slowly off to the east and Morgan could see for miles in every direction. Nothing moved but a hawk high in the sky, making slow circles far to the right.

The driver was a lean old timer named Macklin, and because he seldom had anything to say, was nicknamed Windy. His usually response when Morgan said anything at all to him, was "Yup," or "Nope." Occasionally he said, "Mebbe."

It was an easy though monotonous trip across the flats and as the sun began to disappear behind the far hills, they came into some low brushy hills to the first station, Davison's place. Davison, a big, paunchy man, came out to stare at them in astonishment. "Whut the hell is this! You got a goddamn parade!"

One of the drivers said, jerking his thumb, "We got the President hisself in there."

"President of what?"

"Of the goddamn United States, what the hell you figger?"

"Jesus!" Davison said, staring. "You joshin' me?" He frowned, peering as the President got down,

"Hell that ain't Grant! I seen him in the damn war!"

"Grant ain't President no more for crissakes!"

Davison hitched up his pants as the President and his wife walked into the station. "Who is he?"

"That's Ruther—something—Rutherford Hayes. Whut the hell kind of a name is Rutherford?"

"I dunno, but I do know one thing."

"What?"

Davison looked at the four Concords. "I ain't got the hosses to change. You-all got twenty-four hosses there. I got nine in the corral."

154

CHAPTER SEVENTEEN

Gavin Bowers had been in the room opposite the theater when Jordan had shot the President—and been shot himself. Bowers was startled at how fast someone had fired at the window—and at how accurately! Jordan had barely lowered the rifle when the shots had struck him and flung him back to sprawl on the board floor.

Bowers knew the other was dead instantly. He ran for the door—their escape route had been carefully planned in advance—and down the stairs to the alley, over a fence and through a narrow walkway to the next street. They had left their horses in a cul de sac. He mounted one and led the other and headed away at a lope, knowing pursuit would be quick.

But he evaded it. It was too bad Jordan was dead, but the President was gone too. He felt elated! It had been a damned difficult mission his father had given him, but he had carried it out. He had seen with his own eyes the President step down from the coach and had seen him fall forward as the shot struck his back. Jordan was an expert marksman; he did not miss at that range. But who had fired back so fast! The man must have been looking directly at the window where the shot came from. It was incredible! Bowers was glad he'd been looking out the other window.

He returned to the house where Simon Pake was staying for the night—he moved each day to a new place—and they had a drink to celebrate the quick passing of the man they hated. Later Simon would send a man to telegraph the elder Bowers in the east that the deed was accomplished—they had a code. He wanted to tell Bowers before the newspapers did.

They had several drinks. And it began to percolate in Gavin Bowers' head that it was a peculiar thing that the newspapers did not immediately send out an extra! They always did that in cases of great news. Boys ran up and down streets shouting Extra— extra—!

But hours passed and no extras were shouted. He and Simon stared at each other in wonderment. "But I saw him fall," Bowers said. "Jordan hit him squarely in the back and I saw him fall!"

Even the next day there was no announcement, no extra; the papers printed regular editions with no mention of an assassination. Bowers was incredulous. He had seen the man fall! But there was a story about the President's speech at the theater, about seven hundred people had attended. How could he give a speech if he were dead? Had the security people substituted a ringer? But there was no mention of any other death. Then the man who had been shot had worn a steel protection of some kind.

There could be no other answer. He had been badly outmaneuvered by somebody. Was it Shelter Morgan? Damn the man!

The newspapers said the presidential party was leaving the city to continue the tour and would be in Louiston in several days.

Louiston.

There was no telegraph line to Davison's place so he had not been warned of the coming party. There were rooms enough for twelve people—it was charitable to call them rooms; they were no more than cells, each with a two-person bunk and a few pegs on which to hang clothes.

Those without rooms could sleep in chairs or in the coaches ... The troopers slept in the open. Most passed a miserable night and in the morning lined up at a wash bench to dash the sleep from their eyes. It was primitive living but the President took it in good grace, setting a fine example for all.

Pomfret's rank gave him one of the rooms. He took the lower bunk and Morgan climbed into the upper ... and slept very well. But breakfast was another trial. Davison's cook had never had to feed so many people at one sitting and the meal took two hours with people eating in shifts.

They were not ready to depart until the middle of the morning. And for a while all the coaches and troopers were strung out along a mile of road until they gradually settled in.

They passed the regular, scheduled coach coming from Tamarind. They were an hour or two away from Davison's and the two drivers halted to jaw for a minute. A flash flood had washed out a small bridge but the crossing was not too bad; there was little water in the creek. The driver from Tamarind was astonished at the line of coaches and was not prepared to believe the story about the President being one of the passengers, until the President showed himself.

They came to the creek late in the afternoon, making a slight detour, crossing in the tracks of the other coach without incident.

Locklin's Station was about the size of Davison's, a log and plaster house with a main room, small bar, large kitchen and an ell with a double line of rooms, ten in all . . . rooms very like Davison's. They arrived at dusk, walking the tired horses, everyone hungry and exhausted by the buffeting, jolting ride. The President and his wife retired at once to their cubicle and a supper was sent to them later.

Pomfret's arm had been jolted many times because of the rutted roads and his face was tired and lined; he made no complaint but Morgan knew he was suffering. He too turned in early, with a bottle of pain-killer for company.

Gavin Bowers and Fred arrived in Louiston on the train and learned immediately that the presidential party had left on stagecoaches for Tamarind. People were still chattering about the chief executive's visit and what the First Lady had been wearing. The party had left Louiston a day ago.

Bowers purchased two horses and saddles from a local merchant, laid in supplies and he and Fred rode out three hours after they arrived, taking the road to Tamarind. They ought to make much better time than the President's party.

It was a clear, starlit night with almost no wind. Morgan took a turn about the station, meeting one of Colonel Hobby's sergeants who was smoking a last cigar beside one of the coaches. Hobby had posted guards around the perimeter, the sergeant told him, even though there was probably nothing to fear; they were miles from any civilization.

The sergeant said, "They tell me you were a Confederate officer."

"Yes." Morgan looked at the other curiously.

"So was I." The sergeant grinned. "I was with Bedford Forrest for two years, giving those Yankees hell."

Morgan laughed. "And you couldn't stay out of uniform . . ."

"Army's all I know. Now that we lost the cause,

this's the only army around. A man's got to make a living." He turned his head as someone yelled.

A shot sounded, flat and angry on the night air. The sergeant swore and Morgan started on a run beside him. Someone was shouting, "Post number four!" He followed the sergeant across the road and a shadow detached itself and became a young private.

"There was somebody out there, Sergeant." The man pointed into the desert. "He was on a horse—"

"Why'd you fire at him, Billy?"

"He would'n stop. Sombitch plain ignored me." The lad's face was earnest.

Morgan asked, "What'd he look like?"

"Couldn't see him good, sir. Dark clothes, looked like a bay horse. He come riding toward the lights." He nodded toward the station where lanterns were glimmering. "An' when I hollered he stopped and turned tail. So I fired over his head."

"Only one man?"

"That's all I seen, sir."

"All right," the sergeant said. "Keep your eyes peeled, but he knows we've got a guard system now. He won't be back. We'll take a look in the morning."

"Sure thing, Sergeant."

The NCO went to report to the officer of the guard and Morgan returned to the station house. Had it been Bowers on the horse? It could have been. Who else would run off when a sentry challenged? Bowers or some wandering bandit.

Pomfret was awake when he entered the tiny

cubicle. "Was that a shot I heard?"

"Yes. A sentry saw someone on a horse and fired over his head when the man didn't stop."

The general sighed, "Persistent, isn't he?"

"Too much so. Can't you sleep?"

"Pass the medicine over." He motioned for the bottle.

In the morning Morgan went out to look for tracks and found them quickly. A single horseman had approached the sentry and turned about to lope away . . . just as Billy had said. And several hundred yards into the desert the horseman had been joined by another. The tracks led around the station, into the low hills behind it.

Morgan paused and searched the hills with his eyes. Gavin Bowers and his companion were probably up there somewhere, and might be looking at him this minute. Luckily he was out of rifle range.

Well, what could they hope to do, two men against Colonel Hobby's cavalry?

He discussed it with Colonel Hobby. Should Hobby put men into the hills to find them? Hobby asked, "Is there a chance we might turn them up?"

Morgan shook his head slowly. "If it *is* Bowers, he'll see you coming and get out long before you get close."

"And we'll waste a deal of time."

"Yes."

"But if we go on, they could snipe at us—and a lucky shot might hit the Chief."

"And the sun could break in half."

Hobby smiled. "All right, it's a lean chance. So we'll ignore Bowers and go on. Tamarind is only six hours away."

Morgan nodded and went to find Pomfret.

The coaches and wagons were on the road three hours after dawn. Most of the passengers were in a better mood since the town would be reached that day and they would be able to bathe properly and rest their sore bodies. Stagecoach travel was not noted for ease but was famous for petty irritation; often passengers of a single coach arrived at a destination, not one speaking to another.

Slightly before noon Colonel Hobby stopped the procession. The road ahead wound through some jagged hills. Morgan said to Windy, "Looks like a good place for an ambush."

"Yup," Windy agreed.

Hobby sent half a dozen men into the hills on each side of the road and they waited till the patrols signalled. It took more than an hour and when the signal came they went forward slowly, eyeing the ragged hills on either side. As they came out of the hills the wind picked up, blowing hard, flinging dust and sand into everyone's faces. Morgan tied his bandanna about his face and turned up his coat collar.

But when they left the hills behind and went down a long slope to the valley floor the winds died away and the sun began to beat on them and caused the far horizons to dance and shimmer. In a very short time metal became too hot to touch. In the coaches people rode with eyes closed and few spoke. Soon they would be in Tamarind. Soon they would be in Tamarind . . .

God willing.

CHAPTER EIGHTEEN

Tamarind proved to be a dusty little wide place in the road. It was a railroad stop and nothing else but two saloons, a general store, blacksmith shop and barber. A deputy sheriff rode in once a week if he was not busy elsewhere. There was no hotel but the blacksmith had a stable behind his shop and sometimes let out stalls for overnight visitors.

The stage company had a corral next to the general store, a tiny office and a large yard in which the coaches and wagons were kept. All the passengers got down and walked to the small board depot to await the train. Tamarind was not the Eden they had thought . . . and expected.

Morgan and Pomfret went to the nearest saloon and ordered beer. It was cool, not cold, but they sipped it with appreciation, as the single bartender asked them for news. "You all come from Louiston?"

Pomfret said, "I suppose the best news is that the

President is over there in the depot waiting for the next train."

"You is joshin' me . . . ?"

"No, that's the truth. You must have heard he's making a tour of the west . . . it's been in all the papers for months. Even long before he started."

"Yeh, we heard. He's over there, sure as hell?"

"Sure." Pomfret nodded. "Big as life."

The man took off the apron and tossed it on the bar. He glanced around; there was no one else in the room. "I goin' to take a gander at him. You all hold the place for me, huh?" He rushed out.

The general laughed and bit off the end of a cigar. He scratched a match and lit it, puffing hard. "Glad I'm not famous." He eased his wounded arm. "Wouldn't want people staring at me wherever I go."

Morgan sipped the beer, thinking he felt much the same. Fame must have many drawbacks.

The barman was back in a few minutes, looking flushed. "He shook hands with me! Damn I got to tell my chillun about that! I shook hands with the President hisself! Think I'll by m'self a drink."

Pomfret asked, "Why's this town here anyway?"

The bartender scratched his neck. "Because of the mines. They's half a dozen mines back in the hills. One'r two just up the slope from here."

"What kind of mines?"

"Gold. They taken a passel of gold out few years back. None of them working now though."

"But the railroad still stops here."

"They take on water. We's the only stop b'tween here'n Freeburg to the west and Danville to the east.

That's quite a piece."

"Umm."

They dawdled over the beer, had another one and Pomfret took out his silver watch every few minutes to study it and once held it to his ear. The train was late.

They walked back to the depot and saw the train was an hour late according to the posted schedule. And while they frowned at the posted notice, the telegrapher came out of the tiny office and talked to Colonel Hobby.

The wire had gone dead.

Pomfret stared at the man. "The wire's down?"

"Happens sometimes, mister." The telegrapher was a skinny oldster with a fringe of white whiskers that stuck out from his lean face. "They'll send out a crew from each end, likely. Only take a few days."

Morgan asked, "Did your last messages say anything about the eastbound train?"

"Nothing."

In the dusty little depot, Pomfret looked at the half-smoked cigar, sighed and walked to the door and tossed it out. The President and his wife sat in a corner of the room surrounded by their luggage and aides. Colonel Hobby strode out to the platform and paced up and down slapping his gloves into his hand.

Morgan shook his head. It was an ominous note, the telegraph wire being down.

Pomfret walked outside, trailing blue smoke from a fresh cigar. Morgan followed him and sat in one of a line of chairs and tilted it back against the wall.

The platform was in shade. There wasn't a thing they could do but wait.

Hobby walked to the far end, stood rocking on his heels, then came back and took the chair next to Morgan. "I don't like any of this. Where the hell is the train?"

Morgan looked at him. "If I had it, I'd give it to you."

"I've got that itchy feeling in the middle of my back, same's I had during the war. Something's up."

Morgan nodded. "I know what you mean. We Rebs had the same itch."

"It was a mistake." Hobby sighed. "We shouldn't have taken those damned stagecoaches across country. I tried to talk him out of it, but—" He shook his head. "And he knows he's a target. I guess he knows it better than anyone."

"I expect so."

Hobby looked into the far distance, narrowing his eyes at the shimmering rails. "Do you suppose Bowers has anything to do with this? Him and his goddamned Copperheads."

"That thought had crossed my mind."

The colonel was silent a moment. "If so—what would you do if you were in his place?"

"Derail the train and wait for dark."

"Derail the train." Hobby sighed again, deeply. "Yes, all right. Then what?"

"What did they teach you at West Point? Go after the main thing—whatever it is. Bowers is trying to kill the President. He's tried it already. That's his main thrust—kill the President. Isn't it?"

"Yes." Hobby looked around, glancing through the window behind him. "He'll try for the Chief. I don't doubt that for a second. I wonder if we can protect him in this little building."

"In a little burg like this he'll expect the President to be here, I suppose. Where else?"

Hobby said, "It looks like the strongest building."

"So put your men around it, but move the President as soon as it gets dark."

"Move him? Where?"

"Out of town."

"Everybody? Move them all?"

"No. Too many. All he wants is the President, maybe his wife. I'd move those two and an aide. The fewer the better."

"All right, but where?" Hobby shook his head. "Just take them out in the desert and sit on the goddamn sand?"

Morgan smiled. "No, back in the hills. Don't you know the reason this railroad stops here?"

"Sure. The water tower." Hobby pointed.

"Well, that too. But the reason is there were gold mines in the hills. We'll put the President in an old gold mine — for the time being."

Colonel Hobby smiled. "That's marvelous! It's just the thing!"

"They'll need supplies, food and water. We don't know how long they'll have to be there."

"Right. I'll put Sergeant Knowles on it."

"And you'd better fortify this place."

Hobby jumped up. "Thanks Morgan." He hurried away and began shouting orders.

Pomfret came over and took a chair. "What were you two jawing about?"

Morgan told him what they had discussed and Pomfret nodded. "I think you're right." He paused. "But you found the tracks of only two men back there at Locklin's place."

"We don't know how many he's got now."

"Where would he get them?"

Morgan shrugged. "Maybe on the train he derailed—if he derailed a train."

"Well, something happened to it."

Old Fred had bought more dynamite in Louiston, wrapped it carefully and carried it cross country to the rail line, twenty miles or so from Tamarind. At Bowers' direction he had planted it under the tracks at a curve and had successfully derailed the eastbound train. "Nothing to it."

Bowers had used a glass insulator as a target; three shots had shattered it to bits and cut the telegraph wire several miles from the train wreck. He and Fred had then ridden to Tamarind.

The President was now isolated at Tamarind . . . for the time being at least. He was surrounded by thirty troopers, and Shelter Morgan, but something might be tried.

Fred had used half his dynamite on the tracks, perhaps the rest might be used on the town itself. But when he had reached Tamarind and seen what a tiny little hamlet it was, he had sent Fred off to the east.

169

"At least twenty miles," he told Fred. "Blow up the tracks so nothing gets through."

The westbound train was due in two days, the telegrapher told Morgan. "They run every four days." He had reported the line down between Tamarind and Freeburg. He had also reported that the President was in Tamarind, which news was printed in the Danville papers and picked up by others. Tamarind was a dot, not even included on most maps.

Later editions reported that the train was late, for yet unknown reasons and officials speculated that a flash flood might have washed out the tracks. It was not an occasion for worry, they said.

Colonel Hobby had his men busy building a sort of breastwork about the depot, using a few logs, boards and stones—whatever was handy. The few buildings of the tiny town were all clustered about each other with little semblance of a street, and most were attached, a saving of lumber when two buildings used a common wall. This made the depot more difficult to defend and forced Hobby to spread his men out in a thinner line than he would have liked.

The job was barely half finished at dark. Hobby and Sergeant Knowles had arranged a guard sheet; they divided the men into three shifts for guard duty through the night, and guard posts were decided.

When it was full dark, Morgan and Pomfret sat down with the President and his wife and explained what they proposed.

"But I cannot leave here!" the President said. "It would seem as if I were running away!"

"The country cannot abide two assassinations within the same decade, sir," Pomfret remarked. "It is the office we're concerned about—whoever occupies it."

"You actually expect an attack on this building?"

"Yes sir, we do. Probably tonight."

The President sighed deeply and looked at his wife. "I simply will not run for a second term, Lucy."

She smiled. "I'll remember."

The President looked at Pomfret with a half smile. "It's not the same decade, you know."

"It was for argument's sake, sir. It sounded good."

Morgan spoke up. "It's for your wife's sake too, sir."

"Yes, I had thought of that." He sighed again. "Very well, Pomfret. If you must have your way . . ."

"Good. If you will decide what you'll take—who will you select to go along with you?"

"Francis, I expect."

Francis Waters was a middle aged man, still vigorous and able. He collected food in a carpet bag, found several canteens and filled them at Morgan's direction, and saw to overcoats and blankets. Pomfret explained to the others in the depot that the President and his wife were moving to another location in the town, and to find themselves comfortable positions on the floor for the night.

As the President and his wife were getting ready to leave, the telegrapher came out to Pomfret. "Bad news, General."

"What is it?"

"The line to Danville is out too."

172

CHAPTER NINETEEN

Gavin Bowers lay flat on his stomach, gazing at the little town. The troopers were busy building what looked to be a breastwork around the depot. That building was obviously where the President was. Bowers was several hundred yards distant, concealed in brush on the brow of a hill. He had a rifle in its scabbard on the horse, picketed down the slope, and he toyed with the thought of sniping at the men as they worked. It would delay them and probably stop the work altogether.

Of course as soon as he fired on them, they would fire back and a lucky shot might hit home. Better wait for night. He contented himself with fixing the positions of the buildings in his mind.

Men moved here and there and he wondered which was Shelter Morgan. He wouldn't mind taking a shot at *him,* if he could be sure of the target.

Fred must be nearly ready to blow the tracks by now — he rolled slightly and glanced at the sun. Well, in another hour or so. That would bottle up the

President for a while. He watched the busy scene below for another few moments then shoved back and went down to the horse.

During the afternoon Morgan had had several of the mine entrances pointed out to him. One in particular, he was told, was deeper than the others. It had a long passageway that led to a large roomlike cavern. "There's some bats in it," someone said, "but they won't bother you much."

He led the President, Lucy and Francis through the buildings and up the slope of the near hill. It was very dark and slow going, carrying blankets and unlit lanterns and all the food and canteens. Halfway up, Morgan began to wonder if he was doing the right thing. Was he over-reacting? But damn it, he couldn't afford to take the chance! Bowers could lay up on a hillside and spray the depot with bullets. Not a pretty thought.

It was a half mile march up the slope, fighting brush and rocks that made them slip and slide . . . but finally the mine entrance opened up just beyond a long tailing. Morgan asked them to wait a moment, and went inside with a lantern and lighted it. It was the right mine.

The passageway made a turn so that when the main cavern was lighted, the lanterns could not be seen from outside. The cavern room was larger than he had thought from the description. It was wide, nearly round, and very high. The floor was flat and sandy. The President pronounced it a perfect hideaway.

While the others unrolled blankets and pulled off boots, preparing for the night, Morgan went outside and made himself a seat on the tailing, the Winchester rifle across his knees. He pulled the Colt, opened the loading gate and rolled the cylinder down his arm, examining the loads. He holstered it and lifted the over-and-under derringer from his boot. It was loaded, and he put it back. The chance that Bowers and his men would find them here was extremely thin, he thought. No one else, not even General Pomfret, knew exactly where he had brought the President and his wife.

It was a peaceful night with a high filmy cloud streaking the heavens and tiny pinpricks of stars glittering far out of reach. The ground was still warm from the sun and the lanterns in the little town below winked and glimmered through the dusty panes. It was hard to believe that a man lurked somewhere close in the darkness, seeking to kill another human being, someone he did not know at all, simply because he held a particular office.

He sat quietly for an hour or more, watching the lanterns wink out one by one until the town was dark and he could no longer distinguish even the blur of buildings. Then suddenly a voice spoke behind his back: "All quiet, Colonel Morgan?"

Morgan turned and was about to jump up but the President put his hand out, pressing Morgan's shoulder. "No need to get up. I just thought I'd get a bit of fresh air."

"I'm sorry about these accommodations, sir."

"I understand. We often had worse in the war." The President chuckled. "But matter of fact, I'm rather enjoying it. It's a change, you know."

"It certainly is!" What an enormous change it must be, especially for Mrs. Hayes. The First Lady, sleeping in a cave!

"They tell me you were a Confederate officer."

"Yes sir."

The President sighed deeply. "What a terrible war—and what a terrible toll it took of brave young men. I pray that such a thing will never come again."

"Amen," Morgan said and the President smiled. He looked down toward the town. "I'm told too that this trouble has been caused by Wake Bowers and his Copperhead friends."

"Yes sir, and the son, Gavin."

"Yes, Gavin Bowers. General Pomfret was telling me about him. He's a killer, Pomfret says."

"He is, sir."

"Something will have to be done about Wake Bowers and his group. I'm afraid we've been too indulgent."

"I'm glad to hear it, sir. It needs a strong hand."

"Yes . . ." The President gazed at the sky for several moments, sighed, touched Morgan's shoulder and said goodnight.

"Goodnight, sir."

Morgan got up and took a turn along the hillside and back. He might have been alone on the planet. Nothing stirred and there was no sound . . . until an owl hooted somewhere far off. Another hour plodded reluctantly by.

Then Morgan's eye was caught by a spark of light—where he thought the last building of the town should be, probably the blacksmith's shed. Had someone scratched a match?

It seemed to go out and he thought he'd been mistaken—and then at once a flame shot up, flaring brightly. Suddenly, in a second of time there was fire, spreading like magic! He realized, as his mouth dropped open, that someone had splashed kerosene or a flammable liquid on the side of the building.

In the space of only a few heartbeats the entire end of the building was afire!

At once one of the troopers fired a shot, then another and someone was yelling. Tongues of flame began shooting up into the air and sparks showered, reminding him of bonfires on Fourth of July celebrations. The fire created a wind—that was quickly becoming a monster! The flames reached out for the next building and the wind became a storm.

There was nothing at all he could do and Morgan stood, watching helplessly. Tiny figures scurried here and there. People were throwing water on the flames, but there wasn't enough. Someone had the presence of mind to get the horses and coaches away from the buildings . . . but the town was doomed. The flames were flying—throwing themselves onto other unburned roofs, licking up walls and it began to rain sparks.

Half the buildings were burning—and the other half could not be saved.

The President and his wife came out to stand beside him, having heard the shots. "My God!" the President said. "How did that happen?"

"Someone set it," Morgan told him. "I think they threw kerosene on the walls."

Mrs. Hayes asked, "Why would someone do that?"

Morgan glanced at her. "To get you out in the open."

She took her husband's arm, and he saw her bite her lip.

The President said, "Well, they certainly succeeded, didn't they?" He shook his head. "Those poor people . . . I hope they get their valuables out in time . . ."

The flames had reached the last building now and the entire area was lighted as daylight, with showers of sparks flinging themselves into the air. Patches of brush had caught fire here and there, burning fitfully, then smoking out. Morgan looked about them. Bowers must be out there somewhere, watching, eager for a shot at his prey.

Colonel Hobby had things organized, the wagons were moved upwind with the horses and a rope corral enclosed them. People stood about, watching the flames devour their homes. Nothing could be done to save them. The depot stood a little apart from the others, but sparks landed on it by the thousands and in moments the roof was afire, then the hungry flames ate the rest. Even the platform by the tracks was devoured.

The President and his wife went back into the cavern and Morgan sat again. The firelight faded as the fires diminished, a few hot spots still seethed but the fires were slowly burning out. People were lighting lanterns, huddling in groups, probably discussing the tragedy . . .

The rest of the night was uneventful. Morgan

stayed on watch, dozing lightly now and again, waking at the slightest sound. He was awake when the sun came stealing out of the east to show him the blackened waste that had been a town. Nothing at all was left standing except a few bricks piled one atop the other where there had been chimneys. Wisps of gray smoke still rose in the chill dawn. It all looked like a scene from the war.

After a bit Colonel Hobby came walking up the hill to the mine entrance. "Everything all right?"

Morgan glanced into the tunnel. "They're still asleep, I expect. Yes, no trouble."

"That fucking Bowers has really kicked our butts." Hobby stared back at the ruins of the town. "I would love to get my hands on him." His fists curled. "I'd string him up from one of those telegraph poles."

"I suppose all the telegraph equipment burned up—"

"Yes. Even if the line is repaired they couldn't reach us."

Morgan made a face. "That should cause some headlines. How many Presidents have been cut off from the rest of the country?"

"None that I know of." He glanced around as Francis came from the tunnel and smiled at them.

"Good morning." He indicated the tunnel. "They're getting up. Did anyone save any food from the fire?"

Hobby nodded. "Some. Nothing fancy."

When the President and his wife came out, they all went down the hill. The townspeople had made a camp near the blackened ruins; there were a few tents and several people were broiling meat over small fires. Sergeant Knowles appeared with plates of food for the President and Mrs. Hayes. Morgan went to find Pomfret.

The general was sitting on a box, holding his hand out to a small fire. He looked more rumpled than Morgan had ever seen him, and needed a shave. Primitive living brought all men down to basics. He cocked an eye at Morgan, "Well, he did his worst."

"No, he could have done worse."

Pomfret brought out his cigar case and selected a smoke. "I suggested to Hobby that he send out patrols looking for Bowers. He thought it would do no good."

Morgan shrugged. "He might get lucky. But I think it would take luck."

"Better than doing nothing."

"Maybe. But his job is guarding the President. I suppose he doesn't want to divide his force. He only has thirty men." He watched Pomfret light the cigar with a brand from the fire. Surely they would be working furiously to clear the tracks or whatever it was that kept the train from coming to them. It ought to be common knowledge by now that the President was isolated in a tiny little burg in the desert.

Glancing beyond Pomfret, he saw Amanda watching him. When he looked up, she smiled. She was standing before a small green tent as if she had just come from it. He wondered where her father was . . .

Pomfret winced, easing his arm. "A train will surely get through to us today . . . unless that bastard Bowers has blown a bridge." He shook his head. "God help us if he has."

Morgan asked the general, "Have you seen the congressman?"

"Not this morning." Pomfret glanced about as if expecting to see him. "D'you think he helped set the fire?"

Morgan grunted. "We can't hang him because of suspicion. Even though we'd like to."

The train did not get through to them. But near evening a rider appeared. He had been sent, he told them, by a railroad official to report to Colonel Hobby. Someone had blown up the tracks very cleverly, along a hillside. The explosions had not only destroyed the rails but had blasted out the roadbed. The engineers estimated it would take a week to repair the bed and lay new tracks.

It was devastating news. Hobby, Pomfret and Morgan walked away from the others to discuss it. "The President can't wait a week!" Hobby said. "It's out of the question."

"Then we'll have to put everyone in the wagons and start out just like they did back in '49." Pomfret fiddled with a cigar.

"But that'll take three days—at least. Maybe more."

Morgan said, "It has to be done."

Hobby hunched his shoulders. "It may be six of one and half a dozen of the other.

"No, he's right," Pomfret shook his head. "We have to start moving. Even if it is the same thing in the end. Movement is what we want. Think what'll happen if we sit here in the dust for a week!"

"All right." Hobby agreed. "Then we'll start at daybreak." He raised his brows to them and they nodded.

CHAPTER TWENTY

At Morgan's suggestion they brought the wagons close and made a circle of them for protection, picketing the horses near by. The President and his wife slept in one of the wagons and the night passed without incident. Sergeant Knowles kept the guards vigilant as he prowled from one guardpost to the next, sometimes with Colonel Hobby. Hobby could not sleep; the responsibility bowed his shoulders. If something happened to the President, the army would never let him forget that he had let it happen.

At first light the camp was up and bustling. The wagons, already half packed, were made ready, the teams hitched, and after a hasty breakfast the party moved out following the tracks east.

The colonel divided his little force, placing half in the front and half in the rear. Morgan was on a roan horse, riding alongside Hobby, a Winchester rifle across his thighs.

Two hours before midday, as they were strung out in a long line, traversing a wide wash, the first shot came. It hit one of the mules, one of the two leaders of the first wagon, and the entire line came to a halt.

Morgan yelled, "Five men, follow me!" He spurred the roan in the direction of the shot, galloping hard. The sniper had fired from a low ridge a hundred yards or more to the right.

He levered a shell into the chamber, leaning over the roan's neck. He could hear the troopers pounding along behind him and he motioned with his arm for them to spread out in a line.

When he got to the top of the ridge he could see a horseman far ahead, the horse running like the wind in flat country—and in a moment he was gone, over a rise of land.

Morgan pulled up. It was probably useless to pursue. The man had a dozen choices of escape and it might take them half a day to explore them all. Sergeant Knowles came up beside him, shaking his head.

Morgan said, "He had it well planned. We'd never catch him."

"He's got the advantage, Colonel."

"Yes. Let's go back." He turned the horse.

Troopers had dragged the mule from the traces and another animal was led to take its place.

Hobby turned a worried face toward him. "If I put men out to the flanks *they* may be next."

Morgan said, "It's worth the risk. Tell them to shoot at any movement. It'll give them confidence."

Hobby nodded and went to give the orders.

The line of wagons went forward again, making their own road through the scrub. Progress was slow but three hours passed with no other incident. Then shots were heard off to the left and a corporal came in to report that two men had fired at something in the brush. It had turned out to be a coyote.

"Good enough," Morgan said. "Keep them on their toes."

He rode along the line of wagons, reassuring, exchanging banter and, when he came to Amanda's place, tipping his hat. She smiled and her father scowled, and when he rode on he saw them quarreling.

In the middle of the afternoon he rode out to the right flank in time to see one of the guards stand in his stirrups and send several shots into the distance. When Morgan joined him he said, "Thought I saw somebody on a horse, sir."

"Good. Shoot first and wonder about it afterwards."

The man grinned. "Yes sir."

Just before the light failed, another animal was shot. One of the swing team of the last coach was down, kicking in the traces and a guard hurried to him and put him out of his misery with a pistol shot.

The sniper had been slightly above them on the brow of a brushy hill, but when Morgan and several troopers galloped to the spot the man was long gone. It had been another well-planned ambush. By the time they had climbed the hill, the sniper, on level ground, was a mile away, invisible in the dusk.

Colonel Hobby swore a blue streak in frustration, but everything that could be done, was done. They made camp on a wide plain, so that no one could easily slip up on them.

Morgan said to Pomfret, "There's not many of them, that's sure. Maybe only two."

Chewing his cigar, Pomfret nodded. "We didn't make very many miles today. At this rate we may never get there."

"Tomorrow we'll leave the tracks and cut across country. It'll save half a day. But according to the colonel's map there is a town farther along, not a railroad stop. We'll be able to get supplies there."

"Yes. Hobby mentioned that to me earlier. It's probably another place like Tamarind."

"I expect so."

The coaches and two mud wagons were brought into a crude circle and cook fires made inside it. In the first hour after dark the fires attracted rifle shots; five bullets slammed into the empty coaches at intervals. Hobby's men ran into the plain and returned the fire blindly, shooting into the dark at distant rifle flashes. The sniping stopped.

But long after the camp was quiet, with most asleep, the sniping began again. A rattle of shots smashed into the coaches. Luckily they hit none of the animals. The sentries returned the fire and after a bit it stopped.

It began again shortly before dawn and had the effect of getting everyone up, jittery and irritable; probably the effect Bowers wanted. Jittery people make mistakes.

Colonel Hobby had flankers out at first light and the sniping stopped.

They left the tracks behind and moved to the southeast on nearly level sandy ground. Morgan rode far in advance, seeing no one; the air was clear and crisp with no hint of clouds. With Hobby's binoculars, he searched the terrain without result. And yet later in the day a sniper killed another horse.

They were winding through a jumble of low hills and it was impossible to tell where the shot had come from. The flanking riders had pulled in closer because of the terrain; no pursuit was made.

One of the troopers was dismounted to ride in a mud wagon. His horse was put into harness; there were no spare animals.

Watching the presidential party move out in coaches and wagons from the destroyed town elated Gavin Bowers. Now his enemies were more vulnerable than ever.

Except for the troopers. They were his chief worry and annoyance. If he were not particularly careful they would ride him down and take him. And Colonel Hobby was quite capable of having him shot out of hand.

His second worry was food and water. He and Fred had blanket rolls but little else. The people in the coaches and wagons were better off. On the second day it became necessary to send Fred ahead; there was a little town called Gilead, according to the map. Fred would go there and return with supplies. They decided on a meeting place and Fred set out.

It was not too difficult to find a good ambush point. He could probably only get in one shot before the troopers would be after him, but one shot was all that was needed to kill one of the team animals. If the damned troopers hadn't been there he would have been able to pepper the coaches with lead in hopes of hitting his main target.

Morgan had a discussion with Pomfret and Colonel Hobby that evening. Hobby was annoyed at losing one man because of the shortage of animals. "If that sonofabitch shoots enough horses," he said with heat, "we'll all be afoot, including the President himself."

"How far is that next town—what's its name?" asked Pomfret.

"Gilead," Hobby said. "But it's nothing much."

"We may be able to get some horses there," Morgan said. "There's probably a store or a trading post."

"And maybe a telegraph," offered Pomfret. "With a little luck."

Hobby brightened a trifle. "Yes, let's hope so."

"I'm going to take a ride when it gets darker," Morgan told them. "I'll circle around and see what I can find. Bowers has had it all his way so far. Maybe he's gotten careless. It's worth a try."

"Take somebody with you," Hobby urged. "You might need a second gun."

"No, he also might get in the way. I'll go alone."

"But don't do anything foolish," Pomfret urged. "What if they see you ride out of the camp? They might set a trap for you."

"I doubt if they can watch us constantly. There

can't be more than one or two—or we'd have had more trouble."

He sat by a fire and cleaned the .44 Colt pistol, reloaded it and put a ramrod down the barrel of the Winchester, reloaded it and got up. Amanda met him as he walked the roan horse to the edge of the sprawling camp. Two troopers on horses walked past them a dozen yards away.

She asked, "Where are you going?"

"Out to take a look around."

"It's too dangerous!"

He glanced around, it was dark and there was no one near them. He slid an arm about her waist and drew her in close. She came willingly, smiling up at him.

She said softly, "It's been a long time . . ."

He rubbed her buttocks; how nice and round she felt. He took a long breath and gritted his teeth a little. He could take her out beyond the guard line . . .

No, better not. *That* might be dangerous. He sighed deeply as her hand stole down and closed over his bulge, squeezing him. He stopped her when she began to unbutton the jeans. She said, "Why not. . . ?"

"Because I have to go out there."

"You don't *have* to go!"

He slapped her butt. "Somebody has to. Are you going to do it?"

Her laughter tinkled at him. "I will if you go with me." She stood on tiptoes and kissed him lightly. "I could sit on your lap."

He grinned at her and leaned down to kiss her.

"Adios." He strode into the dark, leading the horse. What a little wanton! She made a man's blood race! He shook his head to get her out of his thoughts. He needed to concentrate on what he was doing.

But the feel of her in the hotel, the roundness of her thighs and the taste of her ripe breasts . . . they made— He stopped short and the horse nudged him. He had to get her out of his mind!

He forced himself to gaze around at the dark shadows lying between the low hills—like the shadow between her legs. He sighed and took out the pistol, turning the cylinder in his hands. He would see her again. He holstered the pistol and rebuttoned his jeans where she had begun to open them. Sighing, with a quick look around, he went on.

He walked quietly for half a mile, then mounted the roan and turned toward the left. He would make a wide circle and come back to the camp. What he hoped to find was a campfire, a glimmer of light from some arroyo or crevice, and he knew that he would find it only if Lady Luck would come and throw her arms about him, to whisper saucy things . . .

But he had to try. Gavin Bowers was here somewhere. Somewhere close enough to keep an eye on the presidential party.

It was chilly away from the fires and he hunched his big shoulders, sighing. Why hadn't he let Amanda unbutton the rest of the jeans. He could almost feel her soft hands on his—He almost growled, wrenching his thoughts away. There was time for that later. He was out in the open now, the roan walked across brown prairie grass and a lump of moon riding low in the east provided no light. He could feel the loom of hills to the right and an owl made a mournful sound high in the charcoal sky behind him. He halted the horse and listened. The clammy cold reached for him, icy fingers poking into his coat. He could hear nothing but the twanging of insects. Then a fox barked far off in the distance and he nudged the roan.

He came to a wide sandy wash and paralleled it for a bit; the sand was pale in the faint moonlight, streaked with dark grass and bristly brush. When he crossed, the roan's hooves seemed loud to his ears.

But not as loud as the shot that came suddenly, a splotch of red flame from somewhere ahead of him. The bullet cracked past, much too close. Morgan shouldered the Winchester and pumped five bullets at the spot as the roan skittered.

CHAPTER TWENTY-ONE

The roan horse jumped as Morgan dug in his heels and ducked low over the flying mane. The shot had come from dead ahead, maybe a hundred yards away. The roan was closing that fast at a gallop. A quick glance over his shoulder showed him he was not silhouetted against the sky. But he must have made a good target crossing the sandy wash. It was a good thing that shooting by moonlight was tricky.

In several moments he came to a deep ravine and reined in at the edge, listening. The dark seemed to close about him, even darker than before. He could hear nothing at all. He gazed around, watchful and tense—Bowers could be twenty feet away, invisible in the night. What a cat and mouse game!

He switched the rifle to his left hand and drew the Colt, pulling the hammer back, the click-clack loud to his ears. Nudging the horse, he moved slowly along the lip of the gorge, feeling the itch in his spine that he'd mentioned days ago to Colonel Hobby. Bowers could be hiding in the ravine in one of those patches of deep shadow, waiting for him to come close.

He halted to listen again. Around him it was whisper quiet, much too quiet. He found himself holding his breath. The roan moved and the squeak of saddle leather was like a screech in the night. Had he hit Bowers with one of the five shots? Was the man lying in the brush, dead or dying? Where was his horse?

No, Bowers was out there somewhere, listening for him, finger on a trigger . . .

Morgan turned the roan, retracing his steps. He halted where he thought the first shot had come from and peered into the gorge. There was nothing but brush and a rocky, sandy bottom, certainly no body—and no horse.

He sat motionless for several moments, then moved on at a walk. And as he moved, he heard the horse, far behind him. Turning quickly, he kicked the roan into a gallop. A horse, and presumably Bowers, was climbing out of the ravine, making no effort to be quiet. Extending his arm, Morgan fired the revolver at the sounds, three, four, five shots . . .

Reining in, near where he thought he'd heard the other, he listened again. From far across the gorge he heard footfalls. So Bowers had waited for him here, but he hadn't obliged. He glanced over his shoulder again. If Bowers had been in the gorge he'd have been able to shoot anyone who came along the lip and was silhouetted against the lighter sky.

He reloaded the pistol and suddenly two shots came toward him out of the dark, but missed widely. Morgan smiled. Bowers was being defiant.

Holstering the pistol, he sat for several minutes, listening, but it was quiet . . . and the tension was gone. The night was friendlier. He turned the roan to go back. What a curious battle, played out at midnight with neither of them gaining anything, nor likely to. Was it a measure of Bowers' frustration? He had not been able to get close to his prey, though not for dint of trying. The man must be raging.

Morgan smiled, thinking how elated Bowers must have been when he thought he'd shot the President at the theater—then found out he had not.

When he reached the camp he gave the horse over to one of the troopers guarding the picket line and went to find Pomfret. The general was sitting with Colonel Hobby, Pomfret with his cigar and Hobby smoking a corncob. Morgan explained what he'd been about—they had heard the shots. "He wanted to ambush me but it didn't come off."

"He's mean as a hungry bear," Hobby said. "It's going to get worse I fear."

There were no more shots during the night. Morgan curled up in his blankets and slept soundly. In the morning, a new day crisp and cool, the colonel got everyone fed and on the move quickly, with flankers out to the sides with orders to shoot at any movement.

Morgan rode for a time with the point, using Hobby's binoculars on every rise of ground, but the land seemed empty. He was looking for dust, but saw none. Dust from the coach and wagon wheels drifted slowly off to the south. The land was rolling and they crossed occasional washes where winter rains had eroded the earth. Cotton batting clouds lay across a sky of saffron and pale blue, turning silver at the horizons.

They halted at noontime on a wide, level plain that was dotted with small brush but treeless. Amanda was walking along the line of coaches when Morgan loped the roan to the camp. He got down and walked with her. "How's your father?"

She stared at him, "My father? Why don't you ask about me?"

"How are you?"

She blew out her breath. "I'm lonely. How long are we going to live in wagons?"

"Till we get where we're going."

"How long will that be?"

He shrugged. "I don't know. We'll come to the railroad tracks again soon and follow them to where the train was halted."

"It's all over the camp that a man named Gavin Bowers did this to us . . ."

"Yes. That's true."

Amanda sighed. She took his hand, squeezing it. "My father says you're the cause of much of our trouble."

He laughed. "If your father is a fool, don't blame me."

"He *is* a fool sometimes."

He left her at her coach and went to find Hobby. There was a dust plume in the far distance, like smoke from a grass fire. It might have been from their pursuers or perhaps fleeing deer . . .

One of the flankers brought in evidence of Indians. A large party had been that way recently, maybe moving a village.

Sergeant Knowles hoped they would not meet them. "Some Redsticks are downright mean since the buffalo have been killed off."

"Can't blame them," Morgan said. "The Yankee government never turned its hand to protect them, or the buffalo."

Colonel Hobby said, "The Yankee government had its hands full with you Rebels."

Morgan smiled. "We did give you a run for your money, didn't we?"

Hobby grinned back. "You sure'n hell did."

He had another brief chat with Amanda. He found her sitting in the back of a wagon, sewing on a dress. He leaned on the tailgate and she looked up, startled, then her eyes gleamed and she reached for him. "Come on in . . ."

"Just passing through."

"You're exasperating, Shel Morgan!"

"It's broad daylight, Amanda Bates."

She sighed. "Yes." She put aside the sewing. "Will you come to see me tonight?"

"That's a long way in the future." He stepped back as a group of troopers passed behind him, most gawking at the girl.

She said, "Promise?"

He waved. "I promise to try." He smiled and hurried to his horse.

The afternoon was uneventful until an hour before dark. Then, far out on the flank, a trooper was shot. There were four shots, sounding flat and menacing and Morgan spurred the roan in a hard gallop, yanking out the Winchester and levering a shell into the chamber.

When he arrived at the spot, Sergeant Knowles was already there, bending over the body. He looked up at Morgan grimly, "Shot twice in the back, Colonel. He never had a chance—never knew what hit 'im."

Morgan picked the binoculars out of the black leather case and peered at the ground to the south. There was an outcropping where stunted pines grew. He indicated it. "The shots probably came from there."

Knowles nodded, standing hands on hips. "This is the shits, Colonel. The kid was only twenty-two, name of Matthew Harris."

Morgan got down and put the binocs away. Two more flankers appeared, staring at the sprawled body. The sergeant was right, it was the shits. And it would likely go on—until they caught Bowers. Or shot his ass off. He would vastly prefer the latter, and so, probably, would every other man of the group.

Knowles directed the men to put the body on Harris' horse and lead it back to the wagons.

While they did that, Morgan rode to the outcropping and circled around until he came upon a high place, one that looked down on the area where Harris had been shot. He found a brass cartridge case in the grass as he stepped down, then three more scattered in the weeds. This was the spot.

Colonel Hobby halted the coaches and wagons when he heard about the shooting. The men brought the body in, wrapped in a blanket. Hobby took the man's effects and troopers dug a grave on a long slope under a milky sky and at twilight, they lowered the body down and the President himself said a few words over the open grave.

That night everyone seemed solemn and somewhat withdrawn. Even Amanda, when he met her, was less effusive. Clouds had gathered overhead and the night was very dark and moody. A ground mist blurred the prairie as they walked away from the others. The mounted guards circled the camp, their eyes outward. They were not able to see the couple in the tall grass.

This time Morgan did not stop her when she unbuttoned his jeans. Her hand slinked inside to capture what she found there as he kissed her. She pulled at him urgently, "Please—I want it—"

He closed her lips with his and her arms went about his body as he moved, deftly pushing her skirts aside—and then she felt him enter. She heard his breath quicken and she closed her eyes, smiling, ignoring the hard earth beneath her. She would have bruises on her buttocks tomorrow, but no one would see. Gasping, she held him with all her strength and the sweet anguish overcame her, wrestling and roiling her . . . and faded very slowly.

Morgan lost himself in the throes of passion, for the moment, thrusting and finally breaking like a wave on the shore to rest in her arms. He rested for a long time, and when he moved, found her heels firmly locked about him, and she would not let go.

Not until the fires burned down in the circle of coaches.

She wanted more, but he dressed her and took her back and they stood for a time in the deep shadow of the coach and she unbuttoned his jeans again as he kissed her.

The next day they reached Gilead. It was a cluster of houses, shacks and tents by a shallow stream not far from the railroad tracks. The engineers had found a better place to cross and had built the trestle there. The train did not stop at Gilead unless as an emergency.

The town was named for its founder, a whiskery man who had long since gone to his Maker. His son ran the general store and trading post — he traded with wandering Indians, giving them whiskey in exchange for pelts or stolen goods. There was no law within hundreds of miles, except for six-gun justice. Sam Gilead was very satisfied with the arrangement.

Sam was astonished at the procession that came into town; more coaches, wagons and people than there had ever been before — they outnumbered the townspeople. He had heard that the President was making a western tour but never expected to see him. The town had no hotel and Sam offered his rooms at once to the President and First Lady, declaring they shouldn't sleep in a coach while he had beds.

Morgan inquired at once about a telegraph line, but there never had been one. The town got its news only from travelers. So frequently it was a month or more late. Not that anyone cared.

They parked the vehicles by the stream and set up a few tents and canvas shelters. A few people went bathing in the cold stream, washing off the dirt and grime of days of hard travel. Morgan went to the general store and asked Sam Gilead about strangers.

"Been a few through here," Sam said. "Allus is this time o' year. You lookin' fer somebody?" He was a stocky man of perhaps 60 winters; he was coarse of manner with strange, greedy eyes and white, wispy hair. His clothes were old and worn despite the fact that he had shelves of new pants and shirts. He wore a pistol on his hip and had a short barreled shotgun under the counter.

"Looking for a man about my age, maybe my size . . ."

Sam shook his head. "Last feller was two days ago, little squirt, ten years older. He bought enough grub fer two and some .44-40 shells."

"Do you have any dynamite?"

Sam shook his head. "No call fer it." He frowned, "That old feller I was tellin' you about, he asked that same question."

That was interesting. "What about the train . . . has it been through?"

"Nope. Not fer a spell. What the hell you want dynamite fer?"

"I don't want it. I just wondered if someone else did." Morgan thanked the man and went out to find Colonel Hobby. The other was conferring with Sergeant Knowles and Morgan told them what he had learned.

"It looks like Bowers sent a man in for supplies. He's probably the one who wrecked the train—he asked Sam for dynamite."

"When was that?"

"Two days ago."

Hobby grunted. "Did Sam sell him any dynamite?"

"No."

"Thank goodness."

Sam had rigged up a pump that used water from the stream. A wooden pipe led it to a cistern then through a heater and the water came out nearly warm to a bathtub. He charged two bits for a bath, which did not include a towel. Most everyone from the President down used it, taking most of a day to do so.

The railroad tracks were about a half mile from the town and Morgan rode out to look at them. The roadbed was in perfect condition as far as he could see. He made a wide circle about the little burg, seeing no one. Maybe he had hit Bowers . . . It was an interesting speculation.

Frank Willis was in Topeka, following the President's progress in the newspapers. The tour, said the papers, was coming to an end. The President would return to the White House—and Shelter Morgan would return to—where? Would he go back to Toland?

Willis was especially interested when the papers printed a sensational story about the President being isolated in some little town far out in the sticks. The telegraph line was down and the railroad tracks had been blasted up so no train could get through. Willis put down the paper and thought about it. It seemed an ideal spot to plug Morgan.

The newspaper had thoughtfully provided a map

showing where the little town of Tamarind was located, and Willis immediately set out. Tamarind was in the wilderness, far from law and courts, an ideal situation for his purpose. He would bushwhack Shelter Morgan and bury the body and no one would ever find out. He walked to the station and bought a ticket for Freeburg.

CHAPTER TWENTY-TWO

A telegraph repair crew, six men and a heavy wagon with materials and a light wagon with household effects, came hurrying into Gilead late in the afternoon.

The foreman, a big, florid man with black hair and bristly cheeks, was relieved at seeing troops. They had been attacked by Indians, he said, and forced to flee for their lives. "A big war party, Colonel," he told Hobby.

"How big?"

The foreman consulted his men. "Fifteen maybe?" His men agreed. At least fifteen, armed with repeating rifles. They showed Hobby bullet holes in both wagons.

Hobby examined them with Morgan. Bullet holes all right. But no one had been hit?

"Nobody," said the foreman. "We was lucky. We seen them coming and got the hell out fast. Jerry and Slim, they fired back at 'em. Guess that discouraged them some. We hit one'r two."

"What Indians were they?" Morgan asked.

The foreman made a face. "What the hell kind? How d'we know? They were just goddamn red Indians shootin' at us."

"Who started shooting?"

"They did," the foreman said belligerently.

Morgan asked, "Did you get the telegraph fixed first?"

"Hell no. Man up on them poles is a damn good target."

Colonel Hobby took Morgan aside. "Can you believe anything they say?"

"Part of it I think. They saw some Indians, maybe five or six, and somebody shot holes in the wagons. It could have been a party of hunters with some young men itching to take a white scalp."

"Yes, I wouldn't be surprised." Hobby looked worried. "But I don't want to risk the President if there's a chance—"

"They've probably moved on."

Hobby squinted at the distant hills. "It might be better to stay here one more day."

"Then send the telegraph crew back with an escort and get the wire fixed."

Hobby nodded. "He asks me about that damned wire every day. All right. I'll send Sergeant Knowles and ten men. They ought to handle it."

That evening late, he met Amanda as she was coming back from the general store with a package. She was wearing a gray dress with black lace at collar and cuffs that made her look much older. She smiled, seeing him, "I was thinking about you . . ."

He took the package. "I can imagine what."

"I don't know what you mean!" She giggled and slid her hand into his. "I'll have you know I went to the very best schools!"

She probably had. But he thought her other talents were natural and not learned in any school. Undoubtedly she could have taught her teachers a thing or two.

He walked with her to the coach and waited till she deposited the package inside. Then, with her arm through his, they strolled away from the camp in the gathering dark. It was probably safe enough; the troopers had been circling all day, some as far as a mile distant, and found nothing. The patrols had been pulled back closer to the town at sundown, but they were still alert.

The land around the little town was flat and mostly treeless except along the stream where willows and cottonwoods grew in clumps. They went that way and found a pathway, possibly made by animals, along the bank of the stream. The water flashed silver lace as it tumbled over rocks and the cottonwoods twinkled light and dark in the fading gloom. Morgan paused and looked back at the town, a few lights glimmering yellowly. Amanda came up beside him and curled into his arms. "It's so peaceful out here . . ."

She was impossible to resist. He kissed her and found a place under the willows in the tall grass and they lay side by side till her insistent hands aroused him. The splashing water chattered away close by and the trees formed a protective canopy over them as her skirts came up and he slid between her knees. She bit his ear lightly and he felt her heart beating rapidly as he stroked and caressed her. Her sighs were sweet against his cheek . . .

Then she gasped and panted, holding him tightly, her body writhing . . . and slowly relinquishing her grip; sighing deeply she kissed him, moaning softly . . .

When he tried to move, she protested and her legs tightened about him, so he remained . . . for a long time. The sky darkened and the hours crept by and at last he stirred, whispering, "We must go back."

She sighed deeply, her arms worming about him, "In a little while . . ." Her loins began moving and he was about to push himself off and rise when a series of tiny noises scratched his ears. He looked up and suddenly slipped a hand up and over her mouth. A shadow moved past them, then another and another. For an instant, against the murky sky, he saw the silhouette of a face — and a feather. Indians!

His body rigid, he held his breath, hoping Amanda would not struggle. He looked down into her wide, dark eyes then pressed his lips against her ear, "Indians."

He could see she understood and he took his hand away. The Indians had not seem them; they lay under the willows with a grouping of cottonwoods close over them and their clothes were dark . . . If they were detected the Indians would surely kill and scalp them . . . but use Amanda first.

In a moment they were past, moving silently. Morgan turned his head slowly. He could see them moving like wraiths toward the town. And in a moment he could hear the tiny bird calls as they signalled each other.

He rose and pulled Amanda up, cautioning her to be quiet. He led her to the stream, picked her up and carried her across, and put her down under a copse of trees. Now the stream was between her and the Indians and he thought it unlikely they would return this way. "Stay here," he told her. "Don't move a muscle."

"Where are they going?"

"Probably to steal horses. Hide in the brush if they come back — I doubt if they will, but don't let them see you."

"Why can't I go with you?"

"I'm going to warn the camp. I may get into a fight. You stay here."

Turning, he went back across the stream as she sank down into the grass. The Indians would steal horses if they could, and they would also take scalps. They might easily overpower some unlucky sentry . . . He hurried, circling the place they'd seen the redskins, and pulled the Colt pistol. He fired once and continued to run.

The sound would alert all the guards and probably waken Hobby and Sergeant Knowles. He halted and dropped down to lie full length; he could hear shouting in the camp, then there was a rifle shot . . .

and another. They were awake all right.

He did not see the Indians retreat. They melted into the night.

After a while he rose and went back across the stream to Amanda. She welcomed him warmly; frightened and cold, she clung to him. Reassuring her, he led her around the town and, using a shallow gully, crept back to the shelter of the buildings without being seen. Everyone was up and chattering about Indians. Apparently one of the sentries had seen them and fired. Amanda was able to mingle without being noticed.

Morgan reported to Colonel Hobby at once, telling him that he'd spotted the Indians while taking a turn about the town and had fired his pistol as a warning.

"What were you doing out there?"

Morgan smiled. "Restless. Just thought I'd look around." He couldn't tell if Hobby believed it or not. But the other did not press him.

The camp settled down after a bit and Morgan curled into his blankets and slept.

Reaching Freeburg, Frank Willis found it to be a good sized town, situated in a low, green valley blessed by a number of springs. The water from these formed a slow running creek that wandered off into the desert and lost itself in the sands.

But despite its ideal location the town was not flourishing. It had seen better days and was barely getting by because of the railroad. The railroad had a roundhouse and a number of sidings and employed many of the male citizens. Frank Willis put up at the Parker House, a ten room hotel in the middle of town. He quickly discovered that the road west had been blown up expertly and was under repair. A dozen or more travelers were waiting for the train, a few of them drummers who made the journey several times a year. These salesmen were loud in their opinions that the goddamn railroad wasn't half as efficient as the stage line it had replaced.

In the hotel bar, Frank met Tim Gargan, a reporter for the *Kansas City Star*. Gargan was a slim, black haired Irishman with merry eyes and a mouth pulled back over square teeth. They had several drinks together. Gargan was fretting because the story of the decade was sitting out there in the prairie and he couldn't get to it—the President was stuck in some little burg because the train couldn't get to him.

"Why can't we go to him?" Willis asked.

Gargan paused. "It's a long way, and they say it's dangerous as hell."

"You afraid of danger?"

Gargan smiled. "You want to try me, friend?" He opened his coat and Willis saw the pistol in a shoulder holster.

"Have another beer instead," Willis said. "What kind of danger are they talking about?"

"Stick up men, I guess. Maybe wolves and bears."

Gargan finished his drink. "Why d'you want to go?"

"I've got to see someone that's traveling with the President."

"You in a hurry?"

Willis shrugged. "The sooner the better. You interested in going?"

Gargan ordered a beer and looked Willis over more carefully. "Yes, I'm interested. My paper would like the exclusive. I hear there's troops coming from Fort Deering. D'you want to wait for them?"

"I'd rather go alone. Troops make rules."

Gargan nodded. He indicated a table. "Let's go over there and talk about it. You got a horse?"

The President asked to see Shelter Morgan, and when Morgan stood before him he put out his hand. "I want to thank you, Colonel, for your alertness. We might have lost horses and men if you hadn't fired a warning shot."

"Thank you, sir."

"What band of Indians were they?"

"I don't know sir. I didn't get a good look at them. It was very dark . . ."

"Yes, I see." He smiled. "Well, I hope they stay away. Thank you again, Colonel."

When he saw Pomfret the general said, "What *were* you doing out there, Shell?"

Turning an innocent face toward the other, Morgan said, "I was only looking for Bowers."

"Hmmm. You aren't still mooning over that pretty

little Bates girl . . . ?"

"Mooning?"

"You know what I mean." Pomfret felt for a cigar and rolled it between his fingers. "All right. What about Bowers?"

"No sign of him. The troops keep him away. Hobby is very efficient."

"Those Indians almost got into the camp last night. Could Bowers do it?"

"Indians are the best horse stealers in the world. I doubt if Bowers could get past the guards."

"Yes, I suppose not . . ." Pomfret struck a match and lit the cigar, easing his arm as he sat. "Did the troopers go out with the telegraph repair men?"

"Yes, they went early this morning."

"Who'll work the key at this end?"

"I don't know."

"Umm. I learned the Morse code once years ago, but I doubt if I can remember it . . . Maybe Hobby has someone in mind."

Gavin Bowers was unhappy with the town of Gilead. It was on the flats without any cover, except along the stream, and there were troopers along it too often, hauling water and bringing animals down to drink.

It was impossible to get close during the day. He had no spyglass and it was difficult to see details from a mile away. A group of men left the town in two wagons, with troops escorting them, but he had no idea who they were. Certainly not the President. If it had been the President they'd have used a coach.

He was glad to see them go. There were that many less to worry about. He'd had no luck trying to pick off the President from a distance; maybe he could slip in close at night and do the job. If he knew exactly where the man would be. Maybe continued watching would tell him. There ought to be a place where he could watch and yet stay hidden — maybe on a rooftop. Surely they'd never think of looking for him right above their heads . . . or right in their midst.

The weather helped him, turning bad. An early storm in the hills filled the stream and swept down over the town, raining hard for an hour, then misting late in the afternoon and through the night. It became a fog that blurred the lanternlight and haunted the crevices.

Bowers crept close, easily evading the horsemen making their patrols. He found the same ditch that Morgan and Amanda had used and followed it to the rear of the stable building where he paused to listen. It was late and most were in their beds.

Behind the stable-barn was a woodshed with a flat roof. An empty keg provided a ladder and he slithered onto the roof making no sound. There was a window overlooking the shed; he pushed it up and crawled inside to find himself in a loft.

It was very dark and he could barely see his way. The loft was a storage area containing sacks and boxes with a few kegs and barrels and some furniture which he stumbled over. When he made his way to the front there was a window overlooking the street. It was dusty and grimed and not made to be opened. He could see nothing through the glass.

He made himself a bed with the sacks and got comfortable. Maybe tomorrow he would discover where the President was staying.

CHAPTER TWENTY-THREE

The President called a meeting of General Pomfret, Colonel Hobby and Shelter Morgan. Why not go on, he argued. Surely movement was preferable to sitting in the little town waiting for the train.

It would be preferable, Hobby said, except for the Indian threat.

"But we have twenty troopers and another twenty people, many of whom can handle a weapon."

Pomfret said, "It isn't that, sir. We don't fear that redskins will overwhelm us, it's the stray bullet that could do the damage."

"I see." The President was silent for a moment. He pulled at his beard. "They cannot be kept at a distance?"

"I cannot guarantee it, sir," Hobby replied. "Especially at night. I strongly urge you to stay here, sir. The train must come very soon."

Pomfret said, "Probably troops are being sent here too from another post. I believe Fort Deering is not too far from Freeburg."

"Yes it is," Hobby agreed. "Troops could arrive at any time."

The President looked at Morgan. "I suppose you agree with that, Colonel?"

"It *is* sensible, sir."

"Very well. Another day or two."

Morgan thought the President looked tired and drawn; his clothes were rumpled and it was probably difficult for him to continue to appear patient.

When they went out to the street, Hobby asked, "D'you think he swallowed that story of the stray bullet?"

"It sounded good," Pomfret said complacently. "And of course it's partly true."

Morgan rode with the troopers, on regular patrols, hoping for some sign of Bowers, but the man seemed to have disappeared. Had he given up, deciding the President was too heavily guarded? It was possible. But when he discussed it with Pomfret, the general thought not. Bowers had shown persistence in the past; it wasn't likely he'd withdraw.

Bowers slept fitfully in the loft and came fully awake at dawn when a number of troopers came into the street below the loft window with a jingling of equipment.

He chewed the pemmican he'd brought along and watched them depart. Across from the stable was the general store. It and the stable were the only two story buildings in the little town. He could look directly across to several curtained windows. They were probably the living quarters of the storekeeper and his wife . . . if the man had a wife.

He thought he could see vague shadows move behind the curtains but it was not possible to make out forms.

As the morning wore on a good many people went into the store and came out; one was the colonel in charge of the troops—and probably in charge of the President's security. The colonel was in and out several times; troops were stationed at the store and Bowers began to wonder if the President was in the upstairs rooms. Wasn't it a logical place for him?

By day's end, Bowers was convinced the President was staying at the store. It was very doubtful if he and his wife would sleep in one of the tents that were erected just outside the town.

Bowers fingered his Bowie knife. He would make every effort to get into the store building that night.

In the afternoon one of the patrols ran across sign that someone was in the area. Morgan was sent for and, with a detail of men, he followed the scanty trail.

As he approached a rocky outcropping, Morgan motioned the troopers to stay and went forward alone, on foot. They were about five miles from the town; the place would make an excellent campsite, far enough from the town so the patrols would not come near.

On the far side of the outcropping was a green area with grass and brush growing tall around a small spring. As he climbed through the rocks, a man came from the shelter of a hastily-built lean-to carrying a rifle. The man looked alertly, evidently something had alarmed him.

Then his gaze surveyed the rocks close by—Morgan knew he would be seen in another moment. He drew the .44 pistol and the movement caught the man's eye. He looked startled, then came up with the rifle without aiming and fired, one, two, three shots—and ran behind the lean-to.

Morgan fired, knowing he had missed. He ran toward the lean-to hearing hoofbeats. The man had jumped on a horse and was streaking away. Morgan emptied the pistol at him without effect.

The troopers came galloping past the green area, yelling as they saw the fleeing men. Morgan yelled after them to take the man alive, but no one heard him. The troopers followed for a mile or more, Morgan heard the rattle of shots, and after a bit the troopers returned with the body of the man flopped over the horse, dead.

He was an old-timer, grizzled and shabby. There was little in the lean-to but blankets and possibles; there was nothing to tell who the man was. But two men had obviously shared the lean-to; the other must be Bowers. But where was he?

They took the body back to the town and Colonel Hobby had the sergeant detail men to dig a grave. Morgan talked to Pomfret. "He was an old-timer, not the kind you'd think would ride with a man like Bowers."

"Unless he had some special skills."

Morgan eyed the other. "You mean the dynamite?"

"Certainly. He was likely the dynamiter."

Morgan made a face. "That would add up. Well, now it looks as if Bowers is alone—wherever he is."

Frank Willis and Tim Gargan, a reporter who was eager to get an exclusive story for his paper, talked till late, deciding to go on to Gilead and not wait for the army.

"It's the biggest story of the year," Gargan said. "I'll scoop the whole goddamn nation!"

They bought two horses at the local livery and listened to some advice, "Don't go that far without somebody else along."

Advice was cheap, Willis said. He could get all he wanted. The road was well marked, hell they'd just follow the railroad tracks. They couldn't miss.

Morgan spent the day with the troopers, riding far afield, hoping to flush Bowers. The man might have seen them at the outcropping where they'd found his partner and would know not to return to the shack. It was a vast land and they could search only a tiny fraction of it, looking in likely places.

For the most part it was a land without water. Waterholes were very few. Morgan and his men rode for miles along the stream in each direction, finding no sign of Bowers. The land was empty.

And then, as long shadows began to creep across the prairie, a trooper stumbled across a horse. The animal was tethered in a hollow barely a mile from the town, saddled, with a rifle in the scabbard, and no clue to its owner.

"It's Bowers' horse," Morgan said to Pomfret when they brought the animal in. "It has to be!"

"But Bowers was nowhere near the horse!"

Morgan shook his head. "The horse has been there for some little while, obviously. Maybe a day."

"That puts Bowers afoot."

"Close to the town," Morgan said. "Is he here?"

Pomfret fiddled with a cigar. "That's my guess . . . but you'd better talk to Hobby. Could Bowers slip past the guards?"

Morgan hesitated. He and Amanda had done that very thing. He shrugged. "It's possible. I'll go hunt up the colonel."

CHAPTER TWENTY-FOUR

Bowers positioned himself near the grimy front window where he could look out with little chance that he would be seen. The vigil paid off when, late in the day, several men came out onto the porch of the general store to talk to the colonel and another man Bowers was sure was Shelter Morgan.

But his heart jumped when he saw the President appear, dressed in a brown frock coat and rumpled pants. The President talked several minutes, nodded, then went back inside.

Now Bowers was absolutely sure.

He snaked out his revolver when he saw the President, but it was impossible. The window would not open. He would have to break it and the noise would certainly alert them and the President would instantly be pulled away out of danger. He could depend on Morgan for that. Morgan always acted swiftly.

He slumped by the window, closing his eyes. So close! An easy shot! But the moment had passed.

However, in the next hour things began to happen. There was considerable activity in the street below the window, then men came hurrying into the stable with lanterns. Bowers barely had time to burrow into a pile of bean sacks and lie like a stick while the men clumped from one end of the loft to the other, poking and snooping.

Were they searching for him? He heard one of them say they would have to come back in the morning when there was more light. Then they left with a slamming of doors.

At the window he thought they were searching all the buildings, at least those he could see. Something had made them suspicious.

He let five hours go past before he stirred. Then he went carefully down the steep wooden stairs to the ground floor. Someone was snoring in the back room behind the stalls; there was no light. He felt his way to the back door and found it ajar. Outside, he looked at the sky, very dark, with no moon yet. There was a ground mist that felt slightly clammy. He edged around the building toward the street and stood in the deep shadow of the porch, eyes everywhere.

But nothing moved in the street; there were no lights, and the town seemed asleep. He studied the blank face of the general store across the street. Two front windows and a sturdy door with a sign above them: Gilead Gen. Store. The door was sure to be locked. Above the sign were two more windows with inside curtains. There was a narrow porchlike veranda on the second floor, extending out over the boardwalk. He might climb it, but he'd make noise.

He crossed the street quickly and waited in the shadow of the side wall . . . but there was no outcry, no movement. He had not been seen.

There was a wide, weedy space between the store and the next building. Bowers went around to the back and halted to listen. From his position near the back door he could see the tents of the troopers and others. To his left were the parked coaches and wagons, and a large corral.

Testing the three steps to the porch, he moved to the rear door of the store and pulled at it lightly. It was latched. But there was a space between the door and the jamb; the wood had dried and contracted. He was easily able to slip a knifeblade between them and lift up the metal latch. When it fell it made a loud metallic clatter. Bowers froze, gritting his teeth at the sound.

But no one came to investigate. He eased open the door and slipped inside. In front of him was a narrow stairway to the second floor.

Sam Gilead opened his eyes at the sound of the latch. It was a sound he knew very well from opening and closing it a thousand times. It was dark in the room; he slept downstairs in a storeroom allowing the President and his party to use the entire upper floor.

Someone had come in the back door.

He slid out of bed, reaching for the old Starr pistol he had carried in the war. With it, he stood up and moved silently toward the door in bare feet. Was it an intruder or one of the President's party who had been out late somewhere? Or had someone come to rob him? He kept no money in the store . . .

But a robber would not know that. He took a firmer grip on the Starr and moved past the stairs and looked into the store, seeing no one. He knew every inch of it and only a glance assured him there was no one there—unless he were lying on his stomach in a corner.

He returned to the rear door and looked up the dark stairs. No one. Maybe someone had gone out instead of in.

But it was curious all the same. He pulled on a pair of slippers and went out and down the steps in his nightshirt. It was a cool night and he shivered a little. He hurried toward the tents and was halted by a guard. "What you want?"

"Shelter Morgan. I got to talk to him."

The guard gave him a hard glance, nodded and said, "Wait here then." He went toward the row of tents and came back in several moments with Morgan wearing a shirt and pants and carrying a .44 revolver.

Morgan asked, "What is it, Sam?"

"I think somebody just went upstairs—"

Morgan said quickly to the guard, "Get the building surrounded. But be quiet about it."

"Yessir . . ." The guard hurried off.

Morgan ran toward the building with Gilead following. He slid inside, looked up at the stairs and pulled his boots off, handing them to Gilead. Then he went up silently, two steps at a time. There should be a sentry at the top of the stairs.

There was. The man was lying face down on the floor in a pool of blood.

Morgan swore under his breath. The man had been knifed. The stairs led to a hallway. There were six doors off it. Which one was the President's? He did not know, never having been in the building before.

The first door was just across from him. He pulled back the hammer on the pistol and eased the door open. If Bowers was inside he would hear it; there was no way to open it silently. There were two forms in the bed, both asleep and no one else in the room. Morgan closed the door, his heart hammering.

Would it be better to shout and make a great deal of noise? Would that stop Bowers? Maybe not. But if Bowers were inside one of the rooms, he'd have the advantage and probably the first shot.

He eased the door open on the second room and stepped inside. The room had no window and was totally dark; he could see nothing at all. The light from the hall was no help. As he stood, debating whether to scratch a match, there was a muffled shout from another room—then a shot.

Footsteps pounded along the hall. Morgan ran to the door and flung it open. A dark figure ran past him and threw itself at the window at the end of the hall which burst outward as another shot sounded. The bullet smashed into the wood just above the window. A third bullet hit the wall beside the window.

The President's voice said, "Sonofabitch—missed him!"

Morgan looked into the hall. The President stood there in a nightshirt holding a revolver. Morgan said, "Don't shoot, sir. It's Morgan."

The President said, "Bring a light, Lucy . . . hurry up." He motioned Morgan to come out. "Someone was in our room just now."

Lucy scratched a match and in a moment came out to the hall with a candle. She was in a robe, her hair all undone. She gave the candle to her husband and scurried back into the room.

Morgan said, "I think it was Bowers, sir. Did he wake you?"

"I wasn't asleep. I heard someone come in, so I picked up this pistol," he lifted it, "and when he came to the bed, I asked him what he wanted."

"Did you get a look at him?"

"No, he was only a silhouette. He took a swipe at me with a knife and I yelled and fired. But I think I missed him. I'm not the best shot in the world."

"Too bad, sir."

"Yes. Well, he ran into the hall and—well, you know the rest."

Men were pounding up the stairs, others yelling down below in the street. Colonel Hobby appeared, half dressed, "Are you all right, sir?"

"I'm fine. Did you get that man?"

"No sir. I'm afraid he eluded us. But we'll get him." He looked at Morgan. "What're you doing here?"

"Sam Gilead told me someone had entered the building."

Sergeant Knowles said, "The sentry is dead, sir."

Men had brought lanterns. The President walked

down the hall and looked at the body. "Damn, I'm sorry about this . . ."

"He's a killer, sir." Hobby motioned. "Get him downstairs. Have someone clean the floor." He walked back to the room with the President. Morgan hurried down the steps to the back.

Saddling a horse, he rode around to the street. Bowers had come through the window, probably dropped to the street then what? A half dozen troopers were gathered in front of the store but he ignored them. Bowers had probably run across the street and gone out to the prairie. He wouldn't be likely to stay in the town; it could be surrounded and searched in the light. He would want to put distance between him and it.

Morgan smiled. Bowers must have been horribly startled to have the President speak to him—then fire at him. The shot must have sounded like a cannon in the confines of the small room. No wonder he had run. He had been at a terrible disadvantage. If he hadn't gotten out of the room the President would have killed him.

Morgan rode for a mile into the prairie, then returned, seeing no one. It was a needle in a haystack search. Bowers could lie still twenty feet away and he wouldn't see the man.

The camp was a beehive when he returned. Everyone was chattering about the close call and Sam Gilead was the center of a group as he told them how he had heard the latch noise then gone to get Shelter Morgan.

Colonel Hobby had organized a search that would start at first light. They would begin with the buildings, then continue outward. Bowers had no horse. Sooner or later they would turn him up.

Dawn was forever in coming, and when it finally arrived men went about methodically searching each building in the town. It was discovered that someone—undoubtedly Bowers—had spent time in the stable loft . . . but was no longer there. Every sack and bale was moved. Every crevice examined.

They turned up nothing but a few stray cats. Then the search looked outward. The most likely area was searched first, the stream. Men tramped through every inch of it, up and downstream for several miles. How far could a man walk at night?

They found nothing. The search turned toward the open prairie. Colonel Hobby detailed ten men for this task; the others remained in Gilead to guard the President from any surprises.

Ten men were not enough to do the job properly, as everyone knew. Perhaps a hundred would not be enough.

Morgan was riding with a trooper, far to the south, when they heard the shot. It came from behind them and instantly Morgan turned the horse and galloped toward the spot. Had one of the searchers come across Bowers? From the sound, the shot had been fired probably a half mile away. When he got close he motioned the trooper to move to the right to cover more ground.

It took several minutes to find the body. A young trooper had been shot in the chest and was dead, sprawled in the dirt. His horse, arms, ammunition and hat were gone.

Morgan jumped down and felt for a pulse then

signalled the trooper. "You take him in. I'm going after Bowers."

"But sir . . ."

"No buts. Take him in." Morgan mounted the horse and dug in his heels. Bowers had left an easy trail; it led straight toward the west. The mountains were closest that way. Bowers had a headstart of only a few minutes and Morgan could see a faint dust haze in the distance. He looked at the sky; it would be dark in three hours. Would Bowers reach the mountains by that time?

CHAPTER TWENTY-FIVE

The trail led straight toward the blue mountains, never deviating. Bowers figured to lose him there. Maybe he even had a destination. The afternoon turned golden and a dying sun set fire to low hanging clouds as the mountains began to take shape.

As the shadows gathered, the trail became harder to see and Morgan slowed the bay horse to a walk with the Winchester across his thighs. He could expect an ambush at any time now.

But it did not come. The mouth of a canyon opened and the trail went into it. Morgan halted out of rifle shot and studied the land. There was greenery near the canyon mouth, possibly a spring; the bay was sniffing, probably scenting water. Morgan got down and watched the land lose definition. The sky slowly faded to a dark pattern and stars came out warily, none eager to be the first. When it was full dark, he set out for the canyon, walking, leading the horse; he would make a much smaller target that way. He had the feeling that Bowers was watching him — or watching for him. The itch was back.

But no shot came to seek him out. He came to the pool, a large mossy pond edged by willows and grass, shaded by twinkling cottonwoods. In the cover of the trees he let the horse drink and he filled the canteen, his eyes on the surrounding murk.

Probably Bowers would not try to shoot him unless he had a clear, positive shot because the shot would give his position away. But that thought was little consolation.

He decided to stay by the pond for the night. Picketing the bay, he curled up in his blankets and went to sleep . . . sure that Bowers would expect him to be alert, listening for any odd sound. Well, let Bowers stay tense . . .

But he woke before dawn and waited lying full length in the tall grass. Bowers might well slip up close using the dark as a cloak, expecting to gun him down quickly. He lay motionless, moving only his eyes, listening, as the sun's first tentative rays came stealing across the flats.

Now Bowers had an advantage. With light, Morgan would not be able to see a muzzle flash — unless by sheer luck he happened to be looking directly at it. Even then if he blinked his eyes he would miss it.

And he did miss it. The shot came from directly in front of him, perhaps slightly to the left, and hit a cottonwood bole several feet away. Obviously Bowers had not spotted him — but thought he had. A second shot came and Morgan kept his head down, gritting his teeth. It wasn't fun to be shot at. Four shots slammed into the dirt at the pond's edge. Bowers must be shooting at a shadow.

The fifth shot hit the bay horse. The animal grunted and suddenly slumped to its knees and a sixth shot smashed the bay's forehead. Morgan groaned. Bowers had put him afoot.

Cradling the Winchester, he sent five hastily aimed shots into the hillside several hundred yards away, picking out places a man might hide. When he stopped firing he thought he heard a cackle of laughter that echoed in the little canyon.

Bowers was sure of him now.

Then for a second there was a pinprick of light high on the hill, a reflection from bright metal. Morgan fired at the spot, three—four times—then jumped up and rushed from the trees into the canyon without drawing a return shot. There were rocks and heavy brush to thread his way through; he began to climb, trying to be silent.

He paused in an hour, estimating that he must be nearly up to the level where he'd seen the reflection. Bowers had fired half a dozen times, shooting at random into the brush. None of the shots came near him.

Bowers, he thought, must be in a good defensive position and would wait for him to come against it. Morgan swore, able to look back down the hillside to where the bay horse lay in the dirt.

Maybe he could circle around and take him from behind.

He began to move to the right, crouched down, taking advantage of every bit of cover. It was an increasingly rocky hill and he had to be very careful lest he start a rockslide. The brush was thinning out also.

A rock came whizzing past him, landing with a clatter. The sonofabitch was throwing rocks!

A half dozen large rocks came crashing down the hillside, some narrowly missing him. Morgan ducked behind a boulder. Any one of them would crush his head in! Bowers was being crafty—it was hard to tell where a thrown rock came from. It also meant he was not far off.

Then Bowers shouted, "Stand up, Morgan! Stop hiding in the bushes!" His voice sounded near.

Morgan fired the Colt at the sound—and Bowers laughed. His bullets rapped into the boulder and whined off into space.

Crouching down, Morgan gritted his teeth in annoyance. Bowers knew exactly where he was. A rock hit the boulder and smashed into a thousand pieces, spraying him with dust. Damn! It was easy to toss rocks down the hill—not so easy to fire them back. He scuttled away from the boulder and ducked behind a thick stand of brown brush as a shot spanged off the boulder behind him. Another sliced through the brush inches in front of him.

And then, jumping back, he stepped into the crevice.

It grabbed his right boot and flung him down. The pistol went skittering out of reach and he dropped the Winchester. For a moment he thought the leg was broken. He swore and moved it—but the boot was stuck fast, jammed into a gaping crevice in the rock.

He could not stand, and was working, pulling at

it, when Bowers loomed up, a revolver in each hand. Seeing Morgan's predicament, Bowers laughed. Raising one pistol, he fired and the bullet ripped at the collar of Morgan's shirt.

Morgan's hand moved toward the Winchester and Bowers laughed and fired again, the bullet hit the stock of the rifle and Morgan drew his hand back.

"You not so high'n mighty now, Morgan." Bowers fired once more and the bullet grazed his shoulder. Morgan swore, both hands still pulling at the boot.

Bowers was obviously enjoying the moment. "So the famous Shelter Morgan is caught like a rat in a trap."

Morgan eyed the other. Bowers was sweat-stained, his clothes torn and ragged from his long sojourn in the wilds. He looked like a man far down on his luck, needing a shave, with too-bright eyes. There was a feral smell about him — it would take very little to make him pull the trigger, to center the shot.

Morgan made his voice sound defeated. "Well, it looks like you won, Bowers."

Bowers nodded, cackling. "Yeh, too bad, Morgan." He glanced at the sky. "They may find your body in a year or two." He was clicking the pistol hammer back and forth.

Morgan said, "I'd be obliged if you'd tell somebody where you left me."

"I don't think I c'n do that."

Morgan timed it so Bowers' pistol was pointing upward. Then he pulled the derringer from the boot and fired pointblank. The .41 caliber lead smashed Bowers' chest and the second shot hit an inch to the right. Bowers dropped the pistol, his eyes rounded as he stared at Morgan unbelievingly—then he crumpled and fell into the brush.

Bowers' horse was tied just over the brow of the hill. With the body draped over the animal's back, he walked down the hill to the pond.

He made a large fire and threw on green wood and branches till he had a tall column of smoke in the still air. In three hours a squad of troopers homed in on it.

By nightfall he was back in Gilead. Bowers' body was taken to a carpenter who made a box for it. People came to stare down into the box at the man who had caused so much trouble . . .

A grave was dug on the far side of the tracks and the box lowered into it an hour before the train arrived.

The engine pulled four cars, two passenger cars and two baggage cars loaded with cavalry horses. There was a cavalry troop and a flock of officials and reporters; the little town bustled with them.

Pomfret insisted on hearing the story of Bowers' last day from Morgan. He puffed a cigar and nodded over the telling, easing the arm in its sling.

He said, "The President wants to give you some sort of a special medal . . ."

"I don't want a medal."

"Be gracious, Shel. Smile nice when he pins it on you. Politicians love that sort of thing."

Morgan sighed. "Will I have to go to Washington?"

"Of course."

"The things I do for you Yankees."
Pomfret laughed.

The *Kansas City Star* printed an item it had picked up from a weekly two-pager south of Dodge City. The body of a newspaperman, Tim Gargan, had been found dead and mutilated a day's ride from Freeburg. Gargan had been accompanied by a man identified as Frank Willis. Both had been scalped, their horses stolen.

Gargan had left a mother, living in upstate New York. He had not been married. Nothing was known about Willis.

BOLT IS A LOVER AND A FIGHTER!

BOLT
Zebra's Blockbuster Adult Western Series
by Cort Martin

#13: MONTANA MISTRESS	(1316, $2.25)
#17: LONE STAR STUD	(1632, $2.25)
#18: QUEEN OF HEARTS	(1726, $2.25)
#19: PALOMINO STUD	(1815, $2.25)
#20: SIX-GUNS AND SILK	(1866, $2.25)
#21: DEADLY WITHDRAWAL	(1956, $2.25)
#22: CLIMAX MOUNTAIN	(2024, $2.25)
#23: HOOK OR CROOK	(2123, $2.50)
#24: RAWHIDE JEZEBEL	(2196, $2.50)

Available wherever paperbacks are sold, or order direct from the Publisher. Send cover price plus 50¢ per copy for mailing and handling to Zebra Books, Dept. 2340, 475 Park Avenue South, New York, N.Y. 10016. Residents of New York, New Jersey and Pennsylvania must include sales tax. DO NOT SEND CASH.

WHITE SQUAW
Zebra's Adult Western Series
by E. J. Hunter

#1: SIOUX WILDFIRE	(1205, $2.50)
#2: BOOMTOWN BUST	(1286, $2.50)
#3: VIRGIN TERRITORY	(1314, $2.50)
#4: HOT TEXAS TAIL	(1359, $2.50)
#5: BUCKSKIN BOMBSHELL	(1410, $2.50)
#6: DAKOTA SQUEEZE	(1479, $2.50)
#10: SOLID AS A ROCK	(1831, $2.50)
#11: HOT-HANDED HEATHEN	(1882, $2.50)
#12: BALL AND CHAIN	(1930, $2.50)
#13: TRACK TRAMP	(1995, $2.50)
#14: RED TOP TRAMP	(2075, $2.50)
#15: HERE COMES THE BRIDE	(2174, $2.50)

Available wherever paperbacks are sold, or order direct from the Publisher. Send cover price plus 50¢ per copy for mailing and handling to Zebra Books, Dept. 2340, 475 Park Avenue South, New York, N.Y. 10016. Residents of New York, New Jersey and Pennsylvania must include sales tax. DO NOT SEND CASH.

ZEBRA'S GOT THE BEST
IN DOWN AND DIRTY VIETNAM ACTION!

THE BLACK EAGLES
by John Lansing

# 1: HANOI HELLGROUND	(1249, $2.95)
# 2: MEKONG MASSACRE	(1294, $2.50)
#11: DUEL ON THE SONG CAI	(2048, $2.50)
#12: LORD OF LAOS	(2126, $2.50)
#13: ENCORE AT DIEN BIEN PHU	(2197, $2.50)

COMING FEBRUARY 1988:
#14: FIRESTORM AT DONG NAM	(2287, $2.50)

COMING MAY 1988:
#15: HO'S HELLHOUNDS	(2358, $2.95)

Available wherever paperbacks are sold, or order direct from the Publisher. Send cover price plus 50¢ per copy for mailing and handling to Zebra Books, Dept. 2340, 475 Park Avenue South, New York, N.Y. 10016. Residents of New York, New Jersey and Pennsylvania must include sales tax. DO NOT SEND CASH.

THE WARLORD SERIES
by Jason Frost

THE WARLORD (1189, $3.50)
A series of natural disasters, starting with an earthquake and leading to nuclear power plant explosions, isolates California. Now, cut off from any help, the survivors face a world in which law is a memory and violence is the rule.

Only one man is fit to lead the people, a man raised among Indians and trained by the Marines. He is Erik Ravensmith, The Warlord—a deadly adversary and a hero for our times.

#3: BADLAND (1437, $2.50)

#5: TERMINAL ISLAND (1697, $2.50)

#6: KILLER'S KEEP (2214, $2.50)

Available wherever paperbacks are sold, or order direct from the Publisher. Send cover price plus 50¢ per copy for mailing and handling to Zebra Books, Dept. 2340, 475 Park Avenue South, New York, N.Y. 10016. Residents of New York, New Jersey and Pennsylvania must include sales tax. DO NOT SEND CASH.

ASHES
by William W. Johnstone

OUT OF THE ASHES (1137, $3.50)
Ben Raines hadn't looked forward to the War, but he knew it was coming. After the balloons went up, Ben was one of the survivors, fighting his way across the country, searching for his family, and leading a band of new pioneers attempting to bring American OUT OF THE ASHES.

FIRE IN THE ASHES (1310, $3.50)
It's 1999 and the world as we know it no longer exists. Ben Raines, leader of the Resistance, must regroup his rebels and prep them for bloody guerrilla war. But are they ready to face an even fiercer foe—the human mutants threatening to overpower the world!

ANARCHY IN THE ASHES (1387, $3.50)
Out of the smoldering nuclear wreckage of World War III, Ben Raines has emerged as the strong leader the Resistance needs. When Sam Hartline, the mercenary, joins forces with an invading army of Russians, Ben and his people raise a bloody banner of defiance to defend earth's last bastion of freedom.

SMOKE FROM THE ASHES (2191, $3.50)
Swarming across America's Southern tier march the avenging soldiers of Libyan blood terrorist Khamsin. Lurking in the blackened ruins of once-great cities are the mutant Night People, crazed killers of all who dare enter their domain. Only Ben Raines, his son Buddy, and a handful of Ben's Rebel Army remain to strike a blow for the survival of America and the future of the free world!

ALONE IN THE ASHES (1721, $3.50)
In this hellish new world there are human animals and Ben Raines—famed soldier and survival expert—soon becomes their hunted prey. He desperately tries to stay one step ahead of death, but no one can survive ALONE IN THE ASHES.

Available wherever paperbacks are sold, or order direct from the Publisher. Send cover price plus 50¢ per copy for mailing and handling to Zebra Books, Dept. 2340, 475 Park Avenue South, New York, N.Y. 10016. Residents of New York, New Jersey and Pennsylvania must include sales tax. DO NOT SEND CASH.